The Abraham Affair

David Hoffman

The Abraham Affair

Paperback ISBN: 978-0-9997645-3-4

To Patrick, for showing me how to write

Part One

Chapter 1

A yellow forklift hefted the gleaming steel container into an unmarked white van. It was backed up to a tightly guarded landing dock outside bunker 471 near the central ammunition depot at Pakistan's Mushaf Air Force Base. An encrypted call told the crew on the other end that the van was departing. The driver and two guards flicked the last of their cigarettes on the ground and crushed them under their army-issued boots.

"It's hotter than piss today," said Atif Azmat, as he lifted his portly body into the driver's seat. The guards smiled.

"God willing, it will rain soon," said one.

"May you live so long," laughed Ali, the taller of the two. There was no security detail to be seen. They drove past two squadrons of F-16A fighter jets lined up on the runway like ten pins with their cockpits opened, ready for takeoff. Sunlight reflected off corrugated steel storage sheds that hid two dozen Chinese supplied M11 missiles and their launchers in a sub-depot below.

It was the hottest day on record, 50 degrees Celsius, 122 Fahrenheit. Two enormous steel doors opened as the van approached the entrance to the tunnel, which descended deep underground, deep enough to withstand a direct nuclear explosion. It was cool inside there. Atif Azmat opened his window. Music from a CD reverberated off the walls. After ten miles, the tunnel forked in six directions. He took the second opening from the left. It forked again in another three directions. In twenty minutes, they emerged into the light of a blistering sun.

"Praise be God!" said Ali. "I get so claustrophobic down there."

The tunnels were meant to protect Pakistan's nuclear arsenal from any pre-emptive attack, but since the American Special Forces raid in Abbottabad that seized Osama Bin Laden in May 2011, the weapons were routinely moved from one base to another to forestall any attempts to seize or disable them. Following the recent terrorist attack on the Indian stock exchange, these transfers had accelerated. The Strategic Plans Division of the National Command Authority, fearful of American satellite surveillance and drones, determined it was safer to keep a low security profile and drive these unmarked vans on crowded pedestrian highways. The Americans, they calculated, posed a far greater threat than any home-grown jihadists.

The tunnel exited behind a non-descript Quonset hut along the Sarghoda-Faisalabad Road. Doors were pulled open and they drove in. Waiting inside were two older model SUVs filled with elite commandos. Atif Azmat smiled as he opened his door. The soldiers in neatly pressed black uniforms got out to greet him, shaking hands, kissing cheeks, exchanging pleasantries.

"I hear you are roasting an elephant for your daughter's wedding," one of them joked.

"Only the trunk, my friend," Atif laughed.

The interior of the hut was like a furnace. They quickly got back into their air-conditioned vehicles. They knew the routine. One of them slid open the front door to the hut and jumped back in the lead car. When the traffic cleared and the door closed again, they pulled onto the highway, the white van sandwiched between them.

With their air conditioners on full blast and the sounds of traffic and the radio playing, they had not heard the motorcycles approach two hundred yards behind them. The cycles, about twenty or so silhouetted atop the Kirana Hills, stopped in a line on a ridge overlooking the Quonset hut, shimmering like a dessert mirage in the searing heat. They were two to a bike, black clad and bearded, the riders in back with automatic rifles strapped to their backs, a few with RPGs. Sand swirled around them, stinging their hardened faces. They waited for a signal from a colleague hidden in the brush across the highway.

A flash of light from the spotter's mirror signaled to the bikers to start their engines. In a great roar, they moved down the hill like a pack of hyenas descending on its prey. "Allahu Akhbar," they shouted. At the same moment a green lorry pulled onto the highway about a mile up the road, driving toward the van and its escorts and another trailed a mile behind. As the first lorry caught sight of the convoy approaching, it swerved into its lane, smashing into the lead car and setting off an explosion that lifted the car ten feet into the air.

Atif Azmat slammed on his brakes and jerked the steering wheel hard to the right, spinning 180 degrees. The SUV behind him screeched to a halt. Commandos poured out, firing their weapons aimlessly. Almost immediately the pack of bikers swarmed around them, firing as they moved, killing them all in a minute. Two of the terrorists jumped from their bikes, hefted their rocket-propelled grenade launchers to their shoulders and obliterated the SUV.

Pulling the van off the highway, Atif tried to circle around the mayhem, a taste of acid burning in his throat, his head on fire. Oddly, he pictured his daughter trying on her wedding dress. Two motorcyclists and their riders pulled along either side of him. The guards inside fired at them, but the fighters in back scored first in a spray of automatic weapon fire. Atif's head exploded onto what was left of the windshield and the van slowly came to a stop in a ditch.

The other green lorry pulled up alongside the white van. Four men jumped out and tore open the rear doors. An oval-shaped container sat on a wooden palette resting on twin rails with ball bearings. It slid easily out the back. It was heavy, but the men had no trouble lifting it. They stared at each other in silent reverence. They carried it like a baby to the lorry, whispering prayers to themselves. As they drove back onto the highway, headed toward Sargodha, a jihadist with an RPG demolished the white van, setting it on fire. A half mile down the highway, the lorry turned off on a side road and drove to an abandoned petrol station where it transferred its precious payload to a late model black cargo van, which reversed direction and drove back towards Faisalabad. By the time it passed the scene of the crime, the motorcycles were all gone and traffic circled slowly around the carnage.

Fourteen minutes after the first attack a helicopter swept over the wreckage of the lorry, the SUVs and the white van, still in flames, and landed nearby. Counter terrorism commandos and a radiological response team rushed to the van. A minute later General Khalid Kidwai, Director General of the Strategic Plans Department, picked up the red phone on his desk, which connected him directly to the Prime Minister. It rang seven times.

"Yes?" came the familiar gravelly voice.

"We have a situation, sir." His own voice seemed to catch in his throat. "One of our warheads has been hijacked." Within minutes they were joined on the secure phone by the Chief of the Army and the Director of Inter-Services Intelligence. The PM issued an order for the National Command Authority to implement procedures drawn up for a nuclear emergency. He told the generals not to inform any of Pakistan's allies for the time being. He needn't bother. They'd already intercepted the conversation.

Even before the Emergency Response Center at army headquarters in Rawalpindi could mobilize, US Navy Seals and Delta Force commandos under the Joint Special Operations Command took off from Andrews Air Force Base while forward-based Rangers and Nuclear Disablement Teams from the Army's 20th Support Command waited for word to launch from secret bases in Afghanistan. Elite Indian combat troops, specially trained for just such an emergency, scrambled jets and mounted helicopters in preparation for an incursion.

Afghanistan, which shared a mostly open border with Pakistan, pressed their informants inside Pakistan for information. Chinese, Iranian and Russian counter-intelligence centers immediately picked up the traffic and their defense forces were put on high alert. In Israel, Major General Mordechai Lonzman, head of the Military Intelligence Directorate, picked up the red phone on his desk and called Chaim Ratner, the former director of Mossad and said, tersely, "The cat is out of the bag."

Chapter 2

He didn't have good days or bad days. He just had days. The rhythm of his life followed the pattern of the seasons. If you were to come across him as he pushed a wheelbarrow along the winding dirt road that led to the red barn or watched him as he repositioned the sprinklers around the orchard with their long hoses trailing behind him, you might think he was a younger man. But his uncut white hair and feral beard would speak of longer years. He was constantly in motion, graceful as a deer, his lean body bouncing with a lilt that seemed to keep time with some inner song. There was a quiet dignity in the way he worked without pause, but the intensity of his silver blue eyes, eyes that didn't waver when you met them, could be unnerving.

He wore no shoes and rarely spoke, except to his dog who followed him like a shadow. His voice, when you did hear it, had the depth of someone who once knew authority. But there were few other people in this realm of oaks and madrone. Besides the dog, a rust colored Chesapeake Bay retriever named Simba, his closest friends were the squirrels that camped in an old apple tree, the foxes that barked at him each night by his outdoor bed and assorted jays, grosbeaks and quail.

When tragedy happened and his life fell apart, his oldest friend Howie had offered to have him caretake this 10,000-acre parcel, which wrapped around a bend of the Carmella River. The land was his salvation. The endless hole of darkness and despair never completely left him, but his grief slowly became something sacred.

On a hill above a circle of ancient redwoods, which the natives called "Feather Mountain," sat a large plantation-style house with a porch along three sides, where Howie and Jennifer stayed when they came once or twice each year. Frank preferred to stay in the little green cabin on the far edge of the orchard.

His home, like his life, was all about simple things. The only decorations he had were the tools he used, each in its own place, suspended from hooks on the walls and ceiling. On the rafters above his bed he had nailed Mason jars that hung over him, filled with nuts and bolts and the little things he needed. It was as if he slept in a tool box.

On the rough wooden counters next to a sink and two-burner propane stove were the model ships he carved out of mahogany, replicas of great three-masted frigates that once vanquished corsairs and pirates off the Barbary Coast. They were intricate things, square sails made of rags, rigging from garden nets, dental floss for ropes; the work of thousands of hours by the light of a kerosene lamp. The soul of a man, he knew, could billow like these bleached white sails, but was as fragile as the tiny canons he whittled from scraps of wood. He was familiar with the long nights of winter, months of hibernation when he would wrap himself in blankets after fussing with his boats, read for hours until his eyes blurred and then stare at the glittering nebula that dazzled in the blackening sky.

In boxes below, the shelves were cartons of books and the detritus of a forgotten past layered like an archeological dig. His current reading, piled on top, was eclectic: crime novels and classics, world history and anthropology, the poetry of Blake and Dunne. There were fewer magazines than before. He had let lapse his subscription to *the New Yorker*, replaced by "How To" publications on pruning, Bio-energetic gardening and the rearing and breeding of bees. Of newspapers there were none. Dig deeper and you would find hardcover tomes on politics and macroeconomics in boxes sealed with duct tape; deeper still and find collections of short stories in languages he no longer spoke, copies of *Foreign Affairs* and other periodicals in their chronological orders, some with his name in it. There were cardboard boxes filled with random photographs of another Frank shorn of beard and short of hair, a few next to faces you might recognize.

There were high school yearbooks and scrapbooks from his time as an undergraduate at Brown bookmarked with pictures of him in mid-air in a red and white basketball uniform and, helmeted, scoring a goal against Princeton in lacrosse. And there were single photos, Polaroids, some which had stuck together, of a clean-shaven young man in a safari hat in a different kind of uniform in a different part of the world with his arm around another soldier holding a joint the size of a cigar. At the bottom was a locked metal file case that protected his letters, a journal and poems he had written for his wife, Joanna.

Next to that was a box filled with spiral notebooks that contained his half-finished attempts at writing fiction. He had always wanted to be a writer. He often thought his caretaker gig was the perfect opportunity. When he first arrived on the land, the pain of his tragedy made it impossible; but after a couple of years he began to fill these notebooks with hand-written sketches of plots and characters and the philosophical musings that often occupied his mind. There were things he learned, strategies he adopted to cope with hardship, epiphanies of enlightenment. But every attempt to share these thoughts—the root cause of his wanting to write—ended up sounding didactic or preachy. When he reread his drafts after some time away from them, they sounded like someone pretending to be a writer. He tried composing in short sentences, eliminating anything extraneous; but it read like a suicide note. He eventually gave up, convinced that words were what prevented humans from the direct perception of reality. This insight became the core of his existence, to shed the descriptions and judgments of the world around him and just be there.

On this particular day, bruisingly hot with not a hint of a breeze, Frank spent the morning cutting up an old madrone tree, one of his favorites, which had fallen across the drive. He hated the chain saw. It scared him. Twice he tore holes in the crotch of his jeans and swore he would only use handsaws from then on. But this was the day he went to town for groceries and supplies, a weekly ritual of shopping at the local organic produce stand, the hardware store and the new café for a scone and cappuccino, a rare indulgence. It was too hot a day, he thought, to forego the power tool. He would be especially careful. The naked red madrone trunk was off the ground a few feet. It would be easy to saw.

The ride to town up the gravel drive and along the ridge of the Carmella River on a two-lane paved road took only fifteen minutes in Howie's '98 Ford pickup. Simba rode proudly in the back, biting at the wind. As always, Frank checked his box at the post office, though there rarely was anything except junk mail. It was a tenuous link to the outside world, but he needed to check in case Howie wrote him, the only way they could communicate. The Internet held no interest for Frank, a subject of constant frustration for Jennifer who was forever trying to convince him of its virtues.

He reached in without looking and pulled out flyers advertising the price of grapefruits and a two-for-one deal on Ibuprofen; but as he turned to dump the waste into the blue trashcan by the door, he felt the heft of a letter. He tossed the junk mail away and stared at the handwriting on the square blue envelope. Not from Howie. Nothing official. It was addressed to him, by hand. He turned it over but there were no clues to its origin. He tried to think who could have sent it. Except for Howie and Jennifer, he didn't keep any contacts from his former life. His parents were long gone, he had no siblings and no other relatives who might have any idea he was still alive. He squinted at the letter, then put it in his back pocket to open later.

Back on the farm, as he called it, he put away his groceries, pushed the wheelbarrow back up the hill to the madrone and spent the rest of the afternoon hauling loads of wood rounds down to his chopping block by the barn, Simba followed, panting with his head down and tail limp as the caldron of heat took its toll. Once the sun finally fell behind the mountain across the river, Frank gave Simba one of the biscuits he bought at the feed store, placed the letter on the shelf by his model boat and started down the trail to the river.

The few hippies and native boys who sometimes hiked to get to this swimming hole, with its fifty-foot cliffs for those brave enough to jump, were gone. A young eagle, mottled brown and white, flew in lazy circles by the mouth of the creek waiting to capture one of the fish that occasionally leapt from the water. As soon as he reached the sandy beach, he stripped off his clothes and dove into the cool, clean water and swam in long languid strokes against the slow-moving current. Simba followed. After a few minutes he turned on his back and floated effortlessly back. 'Not to use unnecessary strength,' he remembered his martial arts instructor saying. The sun was already off the beach. When he came out the first breeze of the day made him shiver.

He lay on his back with his arms open in the hot sand and closed his eyes. Then he looked at his hands, calloused and covered with sand. They were his father's hands, large and meaty, worker's hands. His father was a mason, a man who knew how to use his hands for work and his fists to fight. He never laid a hand on the child, though, and the kid adored him.

His father was more child than grown-up. He loved to play tricks on Frank and his friends, loved drinking and loved women.

Frank had his mother's sharp blue eyes, eyes that could cut glass. She was a devoted Catholic, but Frank's father managed to shield him from the religious education she wanted for her son and he never took to the faith. Still, he loved philosophy and was fascinated by Eastern religions, though he never was a joiner. His parents had reached some kind of accommodation after Frank was born and never fought in front of him. His mother was a strict disciplinarian while his father bragged that he "never met a rule he wouldn't break."

Lying on his back in the warmth of the sand, he tried not to think about the letter, the tantalizing mystery that lay waiting to be opened. Finally, hunger won out, and he and Simba took a final dip before trudging back up the path.

The letter laid waiting where he left it. He could open it, but he chose to savor the moment. *It's probably nothing,* he thought. He was too tired to cook anything and it was still hot in the cabin. The air conditioner Jennifer had given him leaned unopened in its box outside, against the cabin. He cut up the fresh peaches and tomatoes he picked the day before, diced some basil and red onion and mixed them together with lots of olive oil and the juice of a lime. It smelled the essence of summer. He fed Simba, then took the bowl of salad outside to his patio chair and ate, watching the evening sky turn pink with the setting sun and slapping at mosquitoes. After a while, he got up and returned with the letter.

The handwriting was neat and determined. "Dear Mr. Reynolds, I am researching a book on 'The Abraham Affair.' It will be published by Random House, which has published three previous books I've written. As you can imagine, every possible obstacle has been put in my way and much of the documentation has been 'lost' or expunged or classified so secret that only God himself could examine it. Nevertheless, I've managed to piece together enough of the story to know that you are the only person alive who could tell the truth about these events. (I have tried but failed to find Celia Ramirez and can only presume she is dead.) From what I learned about you, I expect you'll have no interest in reopening the past. I can respect that, but it is the future I am concerned about. Will you at least talk with me?

Sincerely, Ilan Margolis."

Chapter 3

A child of the revolution, I have always led a privileged life. I don't regret that, but neither am I proud of it. As I look back now I see it as a source of shame, as a certain injustice. But I didn't choose that life. I was born into it.

The name Ramirez may not mean much to you, but in my country, it is an icon of the revolution. My father was a physician, a surgeon, part of the original group that landed with Che and Fidel on the Gramma. Most of them were killed as they fled into the Sierra Maestra. My father was badly wounded. Both Che and my dad being doctors, they naturally became close comrades. I was named after Celia Sanchez, the revolutionary fighter whose face appears on Cuban banknotes. I suspect now that my father and she may have been lovers. If my mother knew, she never let on.

The Ramirez Hospital in Havana is named after my father. I designed it. It's quite beautiful, I think. I'm very proud of it, but not of my father. I grew up with the children of other revolutionary heroes. The pictures you see on the billboards were friends and family who came to eat and drink at our house. I could tell you stories. We children of the revolution were given the best education possible and every advantage one could have in Cuba. I always had a car and a driver—for my security, I was told. We never waited in lines. When I studied architecture in Caracas, I was provided a lavish apartment and personal tutors.

Though I now see all this as examples of the regime's hypocrisy, I grew up in love with the ideals of the revolution, a loyal compañera. "Equality for all! Venceremos! Independence or death!" I shouted these slogans till I was hoarse. I dreamed of fighting alongside the heroes of the Sierra Maestra, of accompanying Che into the jungles of Bolivia, of defending our beaches at the Bay of Pigs. But I wasn't born until seven years after the invasion, in January 1968, a Capricorn.

I was an incorrigible romantic. Eso es seguro! That's for sure. I lived more in my fantasies than in reality. People have often remarked what an optimist I am. I suppose that's true. I got that from my mother. To her, every glass was half filled. She built a life around denial. Her husband's philandering was just rumors, she believed. "Aren't the flowers beautiful in the Botanical Gardens by the Parque Lenin?" she would ask, changing the subject abruptly. The corruption we heard about was only the jealousy of our opponents, she insisted. Everywhere she saw hope. We would overcome the blockade, the collapse of the Soviet Union, the CIA's sabotage with our revolutionary zeal. Avante! Always avante.

When we walked on the Mercado at dusk on nights with a warm breeze, she would regale me with stories of her life growing up in her native Colombia, magical tales of pirates and peasant revolts, of beautiful women and costume balls that went on all night. I understood where Gabriel Garcia Marquez came from. He was, incidentally, a first cousin of my mother's. He even visited our house on Calibre Street; but it was when I was off at school. I came by my fantasies honestly.

I was a pretty girl, or so I was told, but headstrong. I was used to getting my way. Father insisted on the highest standards, so I was forced to be competitive to win his love. Even as I got the highest grades and honors, though, he rarely acknowledged my success, except in sports. When I hit a game-winning home run against a team from Santa Clara he took all of us out for a dinner at a Party restaurant that only the elites frequented and told me how proud he was of me. But that's the only time I can remember such a thing and, looking back on it now, I think he may have been drunk, mucho borracho.

I was quite popular at school and had many friends. I got my period long before the other girls, but didn't show any interest in boys until later. I was sure I'd marry the first boy I kissed, so I was very careful, too much so. I had a reputation for being a tease, but I wasn't. I only wanted perfection. I expected to do great things and I pictured myself as destined to be the partner of a famous man, a hero like my father perhaps. But I don't like such psychoanalytic nonsense. We make our own way, our own choices. It's convenient to blame everything on our parents, but in my case, at least, that doesn't feel true.

I was in love with literature and read most nights till it was almost dawn. But my real love was math. I was drawn to its order, its precision, its neatness. I almost became an accountant, but my mother threw a fit about that. She wanted me to be a doctor like my dad. By the time I graduated high school, though, I knew I wanted to be an architect, the perfect synthesis of my love of detail, order and precision with my fantasies.

Because of the stature of my family, I was given every opportunity to succeed. Designing large structures for various ministries, I vaulted ahead of men three times my age. But I was good. The heroic side of me produced big, muscular designs with soaring columns and steep roofs.

But the decline of the economy after the withdrawal of Soviet Russia's support in 1990 soon took its toll on new construction and I retreated to specializing in historic renovations. Fidel gave permission to Eusebio Leal, the head of The Office of the City Historian, to restore the old city and other historic sites as a for-profit enterprise, as long as the profits were ploughed back into the ministry. There would be no more support from the Soviets and thus from the government, so the department was on its own. The City Historian's Office quickly grew like nothing else on the island, constructing hotels and factories, producing building materials, tourist services and the like. I was busy day and night. We got the first CAD program for 3D computer-aided design and I became a certified geek. I loved computers. They were the incarnation of mathematical precision. I was in heaven.

I wasn't expecting what came next. I met Jose Fererra at a party celebrating the completion of a large Swiss-owned hotel, that I had helped design, part of the Habaguanex group. Jose had rented the whole Casa de la Musica, a dance hall usually bustling with prostitutes and their johns. The music was delirious, a 20-piece brass band that mixed salsa and rap. Jose was the manager for the hotel project. We of course had met each other before, but always in a formal setting where he was courteous and, I now realize, solicitous.

Jose was considered a rising young star in the Party. He did not have the kind of revolutionary family credentials that I had, which is perhaps what drew me to him. But he was handsome in an old Cuban way, that pre-revolutionary look of jet-black hair and mustache, tall, straight and graceful on the dance floor. He took my hand and kissed it in a humorous way and guided me to the front of the hall where the music was loudest. We danced for hours, only stopping for an occasional rum coke. He would put his hands, well-manicured hands I noticed, on my hips and lift me into the air like I was weightless. By the end of that night I was hopelessly in love. I had found my conquistador.

Oh, how I loved him! He was a slow, meticulous lover who knew how to pleasure a woman. I had enjoyed sex before, but this was totally different. I achieved levels of fulfillment I never knew existed. He showered me with affection. It was only later I realized he saw me as a prize, the daughter of Felix Ramirez, a match that would accelerate his rise to the top. His ambition was as large as his voracious sexual desires. He taught me the ecstasy of carnal love. I was an eager student. I gave myself to him with utter abandon. It was from this place of unconditional love, of pure adoration and trust that my world came crashing down. I doubt that I could ever love like that again.

That awful day, the day my heart shattered like glass, started like any other. I arrived at work early, before anyone else, put on a pot of coffee and sat at my desk. The overhead fan made its usual annoying hum. I looked up at it with disgust. My mind was on the menu for a dinner party I was planning for Jose and an army general and his wife whom Jose had recently befriended. The computer loaded slowly. I went back to the coffee machine, waited for it to stop dripping, and returned to my seat with a steaming hot mug. There was the usual dozen or so email messages. Few people had access to computers and the Internet, so we rarely had the overload that Americans complain about. I had become the default computer geek in our office, so there were always some tech questions to answer. I skimmed through these and then saw a message from someone I didn't recognize. The subject said, simply, *Sorry, but you should know about this.*

I opened it innocently. *I hesitated writing you, but I asked myself whether I would want to know if my spouse were cheating on me. I'm afraid your husband is. I can tell you more, if you want to know; or, you may want to let sleeping dogs lie.* It was signed, *A friend.*

At first, I wanted to laugh. This was obviously some kind of joke. But what weird person would do such a thing? I knew Jose was faithful. We were madly in love with each other. He adored me and I knew him to be a man of strong character, unlike many other men in such high positions. To hear him speak—he was chosen to give the warm-up speech before Raul at the huge May Day rally in the Plaza—you recognized the incarnation of Socialist Man, the bearer of revolutionary idealism. Like so many others, I swooned from the passion he embodied. I'm sure all the other women did, too. It seemed like he was speaking to each one of us alone in an intimate conversation. He projected nothing but sincerity. He was a true believer, faithful to the Party and the Cuban people. How could he possibly be unfaithful to me?

I started to move the message to the trash folder, but something told me to find out what was behind this nonsense. *Dear "friend,"* I wrote. *You either have the wrong address or a very sick mind.* I didn't bother to sign it. Before I could swallow the next sip of coffee, I got a response. *I am sorry to be the bearer of bad news.* There was an attachment. I opened it with some trepidation, half expecting a message from Jose mocking my gullibility. But in an instant his face appeared smiling at the camera, a woman with long red hair in his lap with her arm draped around him. My mind had trouble processing this information. It just wouldn't compute. A sickening feeling slowly spread from my gut. I thought I might pee my pants. I thought my head would explode. I didn't know what to do, or even what to think. I refused to believe it. Someone had played a cruel trick on me. They had photo-shopped this. But why?

Before I could respond another message appeared. *Friend, if you pay attention you can corroborate things yourself. Watch where he goes after work most days. See whom he calls. I have more proof, but I don't want to burden you, if you don't want it.*

23

I felt myself becoming nauseous. I ran to the bathroom and threw up into a toilet. I rinsed my mouth in the sink and washed my face over and over. Then I looked up and stared at the woman facing me in the mirror. My eyes were red with tears. Mascara stained my cheeks. But I was beautiful, was I not? My long black hair came halfway down my back in a braid. My eyes were large. I had the kind of pronounced cheeks that many models have. I wished my lips were thicker, but overall, I knew I was attractive. Jose loved my body. Why in the world would he deceive me like this? No, this couldn't be. Someone was playing with my mind.

I tried to work, but I couldn't keep my attention on anything. Finally, I gave up. Carlos, the manager of our unit, was engrossed in a crossword puzzle, touching the ends of his mustache like a child stroking its blanket, when I walked up to him. He looked startled to see me in such distress. "Qué pasa senora?"

"It's nothing. a migraine. Too much drinking last night. I need to go home."

"Vaya! Go rest." He could see I had been crying. He was surprised. I had never taken a day off before. At home I paced relentlessly around our apartment. I made up every possible excuse for Jose, hoping not to believe the worst, but couldn't get rid of the molten pit in the bottom of my stomach. I was nervous. I bit my nails. I devoured a bag of chips. I considered showing him the emails and soliciting his help in uncovering who the perpetrator of this poison might be; but after much planning and plotting, I made up my mind to reveal nothing for the moment.

Jose came home at a quarter after eight. He threw his briefcase on the credenza, strode over and kissed me, as he always did. "Que bolero?"

"No está mal."

I tried my best not to reveal my anxiety. I smelled him, searching for any foreign scent, but there was none, just his usual cologne.

"Sorry, I'm late," he said. "Work was just crazy. Too many meetings."

He went straight into the shower, as was his routine. He was upbeat, whistling to himself, not like a man who had had a rough day at the office, I reflected.

As I listened to him sing, I could almost believe that he had just come from someone else. I pictured myself grabbing a kitchen knife and stabbing him in the shower, but instead, I mixed us a couple of drinks. The rest of the evening was all an act. The ambivalence I felt before had begun to tilt towards a guilty verdict. I could tell that I was not the source of his joy. Slowly, like a worm turning inside me, I had begun to accept this news and plot my revenge.

I didn't sleep that night and crept out of bed while he snored. Both of our cellphones were left charging in the kitchen. I knew his password because he was forever needing my help with all things technical. Scanning his recent calls and texts, I saw that most were from associates I recognized, but there were several from contacts which only showed up as initials. They were innocuous messages about being late or leaving a key or something. The most recent was from yesterday at 6pm to an RJ. "I'm on my way."

I wrote down these phone numbers and sat at the kitchen counter planning what to do next. Jose emerged from bed groggy eyed, kissed me perfunctorily on the cheek and got his coffee and cereal.

He wondered why I hadn't gone off to work as I usually did before he got up.

"¿Estás bien?" he asked, his head buried in the paper. He did not seem to pay any attention as I answered.

Until that moment I had not thought about my circle of friends, but I realized there was no one I could confide in. I felt strangely alone. I had let all my girlfriends slip away after I started dating Jose. They were now preoccupied with their kids and their various pre-school activities. Thank God I hadn't had children! Was there no one I could trust? Mama would think I was crazy. Dad might actually laugh at me. There was no one.

I went to work and barreled through my blueprints and memos. After lunch I found a quiet place to sit in the park outside my office and dialed the number for "RJ." It rang a long time. Just as I was about to hang up a female voice answered.

"Hola." The voice was drowsy, flat.

I hadn't planned what to say, but spontaneously asked how much she charged. I was prepared to hear a string of expletives or at least confusion. Instead, she replied in a voice that changed to a sultry whisper, "For you or for a couple?"

Taken aback, it took me a moment to realize what she was asking. "Just me," I answered, after a short pause, "Do you do that?"

She laughed. I liked her laugh. "Sure, honey. *Dos mil*," she said, "When do you want to meet?"

I couldn't chance running into Jose. We would need to meet before he got off work. "How about a couple hours from now, say 3 o'clock?"

She laughed again. "Who told you about me?"

"I'll tell you when I see you. Where do you live?"

She gave me her address, laughed some more, and said she couldn't wait to meet me.

I hung up the phone feeling off balance and confused. Any doubts I had about Jose's infidelity were fast disappearing. Back at my desk, I emailed the anonymous source who had outed him. *Friend*, I wrote, this time without quotation marks. *I am curious to learn what else you know about my husband's alleged...* I stopped, thought for a moment and erased *alleged*. *My husband's infidelity.*

Almost instantly he, or *was it a she?* I wondered, wrote back. There were several attachments, selfies of Jose with three young women. 'Ese bastardo!' I thought. One of the pictures was of the girl with red hair and I knew somehow that this was the RJ I was about to meet.

I was nervous as I approached the apartment house where she lived. *Why are you nervous about meeting a prostitute?* I asked myself. But I felt over my head. I knocked on her door—apartment 4C—and heard her walk towards it. She

27

looked through the peephole and then opened the door to greet me. She looked shocked.

"Oh Dios mio!" she said. "You are so beautiful. I hadn't expected that. Please come in."

The tiny apartment was cluttered with boxes. There was a large queen-sized mattress on the floor—a rarity in Cuba—a vanity filled with cosmetics, stacks of magazines and kids' toys lying about. A small bed had been folded up in a corner. I offered her my hand, but she took my shoulders and kissed me on each cheek. Her laugh helped put me at ease.

"You have a child?" I asked.

"Yes, she's at my mother's. What's your name?"

I told her my name was Zamira.

"I'm Rita," she said and laughed again. "Would you like something to drink?"

I shook my head. I felt awkward. There was hardly any place to sit. I looked around. She cleared some magazines from a wooden chair. "Thanks," I smiled.

Rita was tall with a slim model's body. Her auburn hair hung luxuriously over her shoulders. She had a wide, simple smile, lips moist with red lipstick. She sat cross-legged on the rug in front of me. "I'm not used to female clients, certainly not as beautiful as you. Usually they are with a man. But I love to be with women, maybe even more than men." She could tell I was nervous. "Have you done this before?" she asked.

I handed her an envelope with two thousand pesos in it. "No, actually I just want to talk with you, if that's alright."

She cocked her head to one side, glanced in the envelope and eyed me suspiciously, but nodded her assent. "How can I help you? You sure you don't want anything to drink?"

I realized I had been holding my breath and let out a big sigh. I tried not to cry. "No, thanks. I just can't believe I'm here." I explained that I was married to one of her clients. When I told her who it was, she burst out laughing. It surprised me she wasn't more suspicious. This was Cuba, after all. But she could tell the hurt on my face was all too real.

"Oh, Jose. He is so bad. He tries to be so careful. Won't let me ever call him. I know he is a big shot. I'm used to that. All the big shots have their mistresses and they all think nobody knows." She put her hand on my knee and laughed again, that same deep, infectious laugh.

I felt like the room was spinning. Somehow, in the back of my mind, I still hoped this encounter would dispel my doubts about Jose, that there would still be some rational explanation for all this. But here it was, the raw unadulterated truth.

I wanted to thank her and leave, but having opened this Pandora's box, I needed to know it all. She seemed to relish telling me all the dirty facts, like we were sisters. I thought I would be jealous, but instead I felt a kind of solidarity. She told me in lavish detail all his desires, the positions he preferred, the drugs he used. I had never imagined Jose using cocaine. My Jose? But Rita said she couldn't imagine him without it. "All the big shots use cocaine," she said.

I asked her if he ever spoke about me, fearing what she might say. She hesitated for a minute and looked intensely into my eyes. "He never said a bad word about you."

Whether or not this was true, it reassured me. But I had begun to hate him, a hatred that grew like a tree inside me. I hated him for deceiving me, for robbing me of my innocence. When I got up to go, she hugged me and kissed me on the lips. For a split second I considered getting my revenge this way. But I was now out for bigger game.

Chapter 4

Frank gestured for the young man to sit next to him on the steps to his cabin. The heat of the day had passed and there was a breeze coming off the river. 'A hint of fall,' Frank thought.

Ilan was in his early forties, with blond hair that fell across his eyes, shorter than Frank, heavier, a boxer's build. He had a kind enough face, but his jaw was of a man who could be single-minded and persistent. Simba sat on top of Ilan's foot as he petted him.

"I was surprised you'd agree to see me, sir," Ilan started.

Frank harrumphed. No one had called him "sir" in quite some time. "Frank," he offered. He wasn't used to talking with strangers. He couldn't tell whether this would turn out to be a good experience or not. He asked himself why he had said yes.

"I was pretty suspicious, as you might imagine. But I've respected your work for quite a while. Besides, if I didn't talk to you, someone else would tell you a pack of lies. There are people who would do almost anything to cover their tracks." He paused for a moment. If Ilan Margolis had taken the trouble to find him, he probably already knew most of the

31

story. He might as well help him get it right. "I read two of your books, thought they were good."

Ilan took out a small digital recorder the size of a cell phone. "Thanks," he smiled. "Mind if I use this?"

Frank squinted at the device, moved back an inch, as if he were afraid of it, and shrugged. "Have at it."

"Let's start with some background," Ilan replied, with a practiced nonchalance, but Frank could see the excitement in his eyes. "How did you join the Company?"

There it was. This was the moment when Frank could still pull back. He never told his story before. He had thought about writing a memoir, even started it a few times. He often questioned why he would consider doing that. Certainly not to expose anything or fix something, he knew. No, the reason he wanted to write a memoir was simply because he thought his story was worth telling. It would be a shame to lose such a good story when he died. But this was a moment, he realized, when his precious anonymity might fall apart.

Lines from Shakespeare passed through his mind, *The evil that men do lives after them. The good is oft interred with their bones.* He had done some bad things, you might say. He didn't want to try to explain them away or balance them with the good he'd done. Truth be told, there really was only one thing he regretted and it was what haunted him day and night and could never be made right. No, his story was worth preserving for its own right. He knew he would never actually write it, though. Perhaps talking with this reporter would be the easiest way to get it down. Sure, he had signed a non-disclosure agreement when he resigned. There was no statute of limitations. They could come after him if they wanted. But they wouldn't dare. He knew that and laughed to himself.

Ilan put the recorder between them and waited for Frank to begin.

He looked at the young man and down at the recorder. "I enlisted in Army intelligence hoping to land a desk job that would keep me out of Vietnam. I thought I'd end up in Washington where I knew a few girls. After boot camp though, I got shipped to Cam Ranh Bay. I mostly followed after the grunts to assess the results, count the bodies and such. It was gruesome, but I was largely out of harm's way. We got ambushed once, however; the only time I fired my weapon. I think I may have killed someone, but I'll never know." He shrugged. "We called in air support. They napalmed the fuck out of the place and flew us out. My best friend's legs got sheared off. He died in the helicopter."

He stopped for a few moments to see the effect this had on Ilan. The man had heard much worse, he knew. But recounting this story out loud felt good. It was satisfying to tell it to someone who was genuinely interested. He wasn't used to more than the short courtesies he shared with Joe at Ace Hardware or the hippie chick at the natural food store.

"I worked closely with various CIA analysts back at Cam Ranh Bay and one day one of them offered me a job. It felt at the time like a promotion. I knew the war had ignited protests back home and the CIA had become the designated villain, but all that just seemed a million miles away. Once my papers were processed, I got sent back to Virginia for training. It was a relief to be back in the states. I loved Washington and went there whenever I could."

"How long were you there?"

"I was in Langley for less than a year before I was shipped out to Monterrey, California for language training, Russian at the time. I also acquired some rudimentary knowledge of nuclear weapons design and production and was detailed to the proliferation team back at Langley. We liaised with a major general in India's counter intelligence who had sources inside Pakistan's secret nuclear weapon program. In 1974," he paused for a second calculating.

"Yeah, May 1974, the Indians exploded a nuclear device they called "Smiling Buddha," maybe the ultimate euphemism," he smiled. "The Pakistanis went hog wild to match them. I learned from some Russian intercepts that a scientist named Abdul Qadeer Khan had brought Islamabad some plans for building centrifuges, which he stole from a nuclear energy firm in the Netherlands where he worked. Khan convinced Prime Minister Bhutto to switch Pakistan's efforts from plutonium to uranium and took over as the senior scientist in the program. That info got me a lot of attention within the Agency and I was able to land a coveted assignment to Tehran, where the Shah was considering building his own nuclear weapon."

The shadow of a large bird swept across the orchard in front of them. Frank stopped to look up. An osprey. He stood and gestured for Ilan to see it. "Can I get you anything? Any coffee, something to drink?"

"No, thank you."

"Am I going too fast or too much detail?"

"No, this is perfect."

Frank brought out a bag of pumpkin seeds and offered them to his guest, then sat down again. "I lived in Tehran for five years, some of the best years of my life. Great people. Great food. An amazing culture. I got to see it all come down."

"People I've talked to say you were a legend in the CIA for what you did there," said Ilan. "But I gather you were quite controversial. You got sent home just before the revolution. What happened?"

Frank was quiet for a moment. He knew when he agreed to this interview that there was a fair chance a good investigative journalist like Ilan Margolis would uncover this story. Ilan's letter only mentioned the Abraham Plot—different secrets, a different time. But there'd be no ignoring Frank's tale. It was a big enough story in its own right, he knew, likely to get him the kind of attention he had avoided for the last ten years. Seymour Hersh had alluded to it; but without some first-person corroboration, it would remain a foreign policy urban myth. He hesitated.

"We probably should skip over that," he said rather defensively. He didn't like being so coy. It wasn't his manner. But he worried his precious anonymity might be destroyed, if he told what he knew. "I agreed to talk to you about the Abraham Plot, not about me."

Ilan was ready for this. "Mr. Reynolds, I mean Frank. I know about your escape from Tehran. I have it from two reliable sources. I can publish what I know, which will be incomplete; but I'd rather hear it from you."

"Then tell me what you think you know first," said Frank, feeling some anxiety.

Ilan pulled out a small note pad and flipped through a few pages. He looked up and made eye contact with Frank. "I'm told you were recalled from Tehran some months before the revolution because of your complaints about torture inside SAVAC, the Pahlavi regime's domestic security and intelligence service, that was run by the CIA. I'm told you went directly to Senator Bumpers after the Agency tried to shut you up."

A smile spread across Frank's face. He was proud of this, but didn't say anything.

Ilan continued, glancing at his notes. "Then, when Khomeini returned from France they sent you back to Tehran. They needed all the people they could get with the kind of on-the-ground knowledge and contacts you had. They gave you carte blanche to recruit anyone you could inside the Ayatollah's network, as long as you agreed not to go public with your criticisms of the agency. You predicted the Shah could not survive and, after that came about, you sent urgent warnings that President Bani-Sadr would be overthrown, as well. Your memos were sometimes given directly to President Carter."

Frank nodded, finishing the bag of pumpkin seeds.

Ilan continued. "You were working without diplomatic cover, you and ten other agents. The rest of the CIA officers had been withdrawn just before they took our hostages at the Embassy. What did you do?"

Frank smiled. 'This guy already knows most of the story,' he thought. 'No use bullshitting him. If he knows this much about Tehran, he probably knows about the Abraham Plot, too.'

"Well, Ilan," he began. "You've done your homework. Except for that Hersh speculation in the *New Yorker*, that story's never been told. I guess enough time has passed for it to come out now. I'll tell you everything you want to know. I won't hide a thing, but I want your agreement that this is off-the-record, at least for now. We can decide later what parts you can quote. Do I have your word?"

They shook hands. Frank proceeded to tell how he and his team eluded capture, how a group of Carmelite Nuns hid them in a tomb under a monastery among the coffins of ancient sages, and how they managed to escape in nun's habits.

It was hard to see this bearded off-the-grid mountain man, who sat straight as a yoga instructor, being the clandestine CIA agent in this story. "Where'd you go when you escaped?" asked Ilan.

"We were in Sana and then Riyadh. Ironically, we arrived on November 20, '79, the day that a Saudi preacher named Juhaymanal Uteybi stormed the Grand Mosque in Mecca and took a hundred thousand worshippers prisoner, an event which, you could say, marked the origins of Al Qaeda. It took everyone by surprise. It required weeks to root them out. Hundreds were killed. The Saudis managed to keep reports to a minimum while the world mostly focused on Tehran and the American hostages. They effectively brushed-stroked this from the history books and it has largely been forgotten."

I asked to stay on in Riyadh, even though I hadn't slept for days, and I was able to go along with some Saudi National Guard troops when they stormed the tunnels underneath the mosque. It was a bloodbath on both sides. I tried to convince Langley the Jihadists in Mecca represented a bigger long-term threat than the mullahs in Tehran, but no on in Washington wanted to hear that."

"What happened then?"

"When no one listened, I leaked information to a British newspaper and some members of Congress. Langley was not pleased. I got busted again, sent back to a desk job as an analyst."

"When did you return to the field?"

Frank looked up at the sky for a moment. Memories from those years flooded his mind. Lebanon, January 1982. A memo he wrote to say that the Israelis were planning to invade Lebanon got the attention of Secretary of State Haig, who warned President Reagan. Haig sent Frank back to the field to help John Mroz, the Secretary's secret emissary to the PLO. Leaving a hotel in Beirut one afternoon, someone warned them not to get in the lead car. Minutes later an Israeli jet swooped down and destroyed the car in a missile attack.

"Frank?" Ilan said, waking him from his reverie.

He continued like this, telling story after story, four decades from the front lines. They talked for two hours straight without a break. Frank walked him by the big house and made a pot of tea. They sat out on the deck and watched the sun cast its shadows across the river. A half-dozen hawks circled in formation. Ilan took out his recorder again and they resumed.

The weight of so much history, a lifetime engaged with events of such huge consequence, made Frank think how lucky he was to have experienced all this. But he also felt exposed in ways he had avoided for so long. He wished his simple, private life could just go on forever. He wished in many ways he hadn't agreed to this interview. He wished he could get up tomorrow morning to watch the sun rise and go through the same routine he did every day without a thought or care about the outside world—just he and Simba. But he knew it wasn't as simple as that. 'Better to be ensnared by the truth than a bunch of lies,' he thought.

Chapter 5

"Tell me how you met Celia Ramirez," Ilan began again.

Frank smiled. "I didn't actually meet her at first, not in person, I mean. Believe it or not, I first contacted her by email." He laughed at how different his life was then, how much of a Luddite he had become. "The Internet was something new for Cuba. Only the elites had access to it. But we had our own ways to get online. We wanted to get an ear on her husband, Jose Fererra, who was being groomed for a leadership position in the Party. We had damaging information about him, but we didn't necessarily want to expose him until we could get the most out of it. Instead, I thought we might use this dirt to turn his wife. It was a delicate operation because we wanted her to stay with him, but be mad enough to feed us information. If she left him, we'd blow our source. Frankly, looking back, it seems like a stupid idea that had little chance of success. But we were lucky."

"So, exactly what did you do?"

"I started by sending her photographs of Jose with one of the prostitutes he frequented, then others. But I held back telling her about the bribes he was taking from a Swiss construction company whose licenses he controlled. He was getting rich; but in Cuba there weren't many ways to spend lavishly except on cocaine and whores, which he indulged in regularly. There was a whole culture of corruption in some corners of the Party and the military, but it was never ostentatious. Jose was good at keeping a low profile in his private life while he took every opportunity to inflate his public one. What he didn't spend on drugs and sex he had deposited in secret Swiss bank accounts. Jose's life was one big party."

Ilan asked if he could smoke and took out a pack, offering one to Frank.

Frank shook his head. "I used to smoke constantly when I was a field agent. Don't know how I could have done it without smoking. It was an important way to bond with my sources. They'd have more confidence in me, if we shared vices." He smiled. "There were quite a few of those. But now I'm as clean as a baby lamb."

Ilan gestured for him to continue.

"Celia surprised us. She went to meet one of the prostitutes Jose was seeing. At first it was to convince herself of his guilt, but it turned into something else we hadn't expected. My plan was to gain her confidence and slowly get her to provide us innocuous information about her husband—whom he met with, where he travelled, things we already knew. As we gradually exposed more of his crimes and indiscretions, we hoped we could get her to reveal more important secrets. But things escalated faster than we anticipated. You know the quote,

There is no fury like a woman scorned. For Celia it was not just her husband's infidelities, though; it was everything she had believed in: her mother and father, the idealism of the revolution and the man she gave herself to body and soul. The deception was total."

"When I informed her about the jewelry, the lingerie and the presents Jose gave his favorite escorts, she asked how he could afford such things. So, I slowly fed her information about his secret bank accounts and the corruption he engaged in. If it were just Jose, of course, she could blame one very bad apple; but we told her about others, people she knew whom she had respected, leaders of the Party, icons of the revolution. Her radicalization was swift. She was eager to learn more. She began to request books and articles by Cuban dissidents and started to see things through different eyes. The hypocrisy cut like steel. Even her father was not spared. He left his own trail of philandering. This was perhaps the worst blow for her, or perhaps when she realized her mother turned a blind eye to it and to her husband's petty corruptions."

"But what finally turned Celia and got her to cooperate was an incident involving one of the prostitutes Jose frequented, a young dark-skinned girl named Eterio whom Celia had secretly befriended. One of Eterio's clients was a general, a friend of Jose's, who got too rough with her, beat her badly. Celia was horrified when the Party covered it up. The local block captain of the Committee for the Defense of the Revolution threatened to send Eterio to prison and take away the house where she lived, if she spoke to anyone about it. There was no place for her to complain. One night, Celia overheard Jose laughing about the incident. That did it. She turned on the regime and never looked back."

Ilan lit another cigarette. He leaned closer to Frank.

"In many ways what Celia was experiencing was like what many American kids went through in the Sixties—anger at being lied to, mistrust of institutions they had once believed in, bitterness at the hypocrisy of the generation that raised them," said Ilan. "But it is one thing to have your eyes opened and quite another to actively betray your government."

"I think she suspected I was with American intelligence," Frank answered, "but she didn't ask. The quid pro quo for the bits of information she provided was an exchange of damaging stories about sex and corruption among the friends and colleagues of her husband and her father. I never asked her for any state secrets, though I was being pressured by Langley to do so. Then, one day, she demanded to meet with me. Of course, there was no way I could safely go to Cuba to see her. But we arranged for her to be invited to an architectural conference in Monterrey, Mexico and we agreed to meet there."

"A hundred-dollar bill and a wink got me an adjoining suite next to hers," Frank continued. "While she was at the conference we swept both of our rooms to make sure there were no bugs, then planted our own secret camera in hers. When she returned to her room that afternoon, I knocked at the door between us and she let me in. I had seen plenty of photos of her, but I was unprepared for the sheer magnetism of her smile. She was a classic Latin beauty with strong, intelligent eyes. The new Celia had dropped any hint of her former innocence and naiveté. I knew immediately that anything short of total candor, of complete transparency, would lose her confidence."

"'At last we meet.' She smiled and held out her hand, then gestured for us to sit on the chairs. 'What should I call you, my friend?' she asked, laughing at the anonymous greeting I had used in all of our emails."

"I told her to call me Mark. 'But that's not my real name,' I admitted right off, without waiting for her to ask."

"She got very quiet. The smile disappeared from her face and she scrutinized me carefully. 'So, who are you then?'"

"I told her frankly that I was an American intelligence officer, that, like her, I had once believed in the Cuban revolution and only hoped to see its ideals realized."

Ilan raised his eyebrows questioningly.

"I did. But that's another story," Frank said. "She asked whether our conversation was being recorded. I told her it was. She winced, but didn't ask me to leave. Our conversation was formal, businesslike after that. I told her we wanted only to know the extent of corruption among the leading cadres. There were plenty of patriotic Cubans, like herself, who deserved better."

"'Don't patronize me,' she said. 'Perhaps we want the same thing, but I'm the one who would be executed for speaking with an American CIA agent.'"

"I'll never forget the look she gave me then. We stared at each other in silence, our eyes acknowledging the grave truth of what she had said. Finally, she asked, 'What do I get out of this?'"

"'What do you want?' I answered."

"She reflected for a moment and then said, 'I want your word that you will never use any of what you learn from me without my prior consent. I want a guarantee that, if I decide to leave my husband and defect from Cuba, you will provide me with a safe escape and a house paid for and a stipend to start my life again.' She paused for a moment. 'These prostitutes know everything about my country. The government likes to deny it has a prostitution problem, but it does. These girls are getting screwed.' She laughed. 'Excuse the pun. They have no rights, no dignity. I want to be able to pay them something whenever we meet. They could be a source of great information. They know more than anyone.'"

"She stood up and offered her hand."

"'We have a deal then,' I said."

She held onto my hand. Then she stood on tiptoes and whispered in my ear, 'Could we talk again without any microphones?'"

"I suggested we meet on the beach at the Punta Resort during the lunch break tomorrow. She shook hands again and I left."

"What happened after that?" Ilan asked.

"After that, we met and walked on the beach in our bare feet and had a long talk about our lives. The conference was large. She assured me she wouldn't be missed. We walked for three or four hours."

"'Tell me,' she said. 'Do all men cheat on their wives?' I was not expecting that."

"I stopped and looked at her directly. 'Not all men,' I said. I could tell what she was thinking. 'I am very happily married,' I told her. 'I would never cheat on my wife. Even if she never found out, I would know I had deceived her. I would have broken something sacred between us. Nothing could be worth that.'"

"I could tell my sincerity made an impression on her. I think she was looking for something to believe in. She told me she didn't think she could ever love again. The pain cut too deep. 'Your wife is very lucky,' she said. 'I hope I get a chance someday to meet her.'"

"We talked about her dreams. She wanted to start a business, she said. Everyone wanted to do that now with the reforms that were grudgingly being introduced. She had childhood friends who had gone to America and she hoped someday to see them again."

"I told her it would be easy to arrange that."

"'I'm sick of politics,' she said. "It's all a pack of lies, in your country, in Cuba, everywhere. It's all about money.'

"I told her my philosophy about intelligence work. 'It's the same as journalism or science,' I said. 'It should be as objective as possible. Our job is to give policy makers the most accurate information we can.'"

"'And expose lies,' she said."

"Yes."

"She stopped again and faced me. 'Tell me your own dreams,' she asked."

"I smiled. They were very simple. 'My wife and I talk all the time of quitting the rat race, going off the grid, just living on the land.' Frank motioned outside. "I told her, 'I have a friend who owns a huge track of land in Northern California on the Carmella River they call Feather Mountain. We dream about moving there after we both retire,' I admitted."

"I could tell she trusted me. She had no one else. I gave her a USB flash drive that had encryption software she could use so we could correspond. I told her I'd arrange a cash drop for her to pay something to the prostitutes she met. We agreed to be in touch."

"Over the next few months she provided regular information about the habits of some of the most senior officials in Cuba, even some visiting Russian and Venezuelan businessmen and politicians. The money we paid to her and her informants was a pittance. We could hardly believe how easy and almost cost-free this was."

"Then one day she asked to see me again. Her husband was going on a business trip to Venezuela, she said, and she planned to accompany him. We met on a hiking trail on Avila Mountain on the northern edge of the city. She rode the Teleferico to the top with its magnificent views of Caracas. We made sure she wasn't being followed. She trailed one of my agents to a side path largely overgrown with Manzanita. I was waiting for her. We kissed casually on both cheeks like old friends. For a half hour or so we just talked about my travels.

She wanted to know about all the places my wife and I had visited. Which countries did she like the most? That sort of thing."

"Finally, she said, 'I'm going to start a business.'"

"I smiled with enthusiasm. 'What do you have in mind?' I asked. She stared intently at me. 'I'm going to start a non-governmental intelligence agency. You Americans have non-governmental organizations for everything: election monitoring, foreign policy, media, public health, development, you name it. But what about an independent intelligence agency?'"

"I laughed before realizing she was quite serious. 'Will this be a non-profit NGO?'"

"'Not exactly,' she said. 'It will be a cooperative, Cuban style. I will share all the profits with my employees.'"

"'Who will you hire?' I asked, now deeply intrigued."

"'Prostitutes, of course,' she answered with some pride. 'I'm organizing them.' She looked at me with a devious smile. 'It's all well and good to get the token funds you've provided. We are most grateful. But this is the new Cuba. One must be an entrepreneur, a clever businesswoman.' She handed me a flash drive. 'You'll find this information quite valuable, I think. If you want more like this, it will cost you $25,000. There's a list of some of the clients our organization is servicing. You'll be impressed. If you have specific questions you'd like answered, we'd be happy to give you a quote.'"

Chapter 6

Once I returned to Havana, the "business" took off faster than we could have imagined. The girls had been moved to tears when I had given them a couple hundred dollars for the relatively harmless information they gleaned from their hundred-dollar tricks. But with our new business, they became adept at coaxing weightier secrets that earned them thousands. Their johns loved to talk about themselves and the even more powerful people they knew. It was hard to get them to stop. They might lie to their wives, but they were the paradigm of honesty with their lovers. I've never understood why governments use torture. Turns out it's quite simple to get men to talk: the more important they are the easier.

The biggest threat we faced was success. Nothing attracts more attention in Cuba than wealth. We talked about this endlessly and decided to put the bulk of our earnings in safe, offshore bank accounts. All the girls planned to escape the island someday once they accumulated enough of a nest egg. I, too, began to plan for a future elsewhere. I had no illusions about America. We Cubans know all about life in the states.

We all have relatives there, we watch American television shows and we are constantly reminded of the dark side of the imperialist enemy, which has threatened us since independence. I could easily imagine living there, though. As a Cuban, I only had to set foot in the states to get citizenship. But I could also live in Spain or France or anywhere I desired. Dreaming about this future got me to consider expanding my business. There were prostitutes everywhere. Why not set up shop wherever there were secrets, men and money?

I was also feeling increasingly lonely. As I withdrew from Jose, I slowly separated myself from our circle of friends. The secrets that were at the core of my everyday life required a vigilance and reserve that changed how I acted around people. Even at work I turned inward. There was no one I could confide in except my sex-worker partners. I missed the intellectual stimulation of my former friends. I began to feel like I was suffocating. I longed to be my true self.

My desire for revenge, which started me on this path, seemed insufficient. I could embarrass Jose, perhaps even put a dent in his career; but I knew he'd survive. I would be the one who suffered the most. He was one of them. The system would excuse him, cover things up, protect its own. Besides, revenge kept me tied to him emotionally. I wanted out. When one of Jose's whoring buddies, a disgusting army officer named Carlos, beat one of my prostitutes unconscious, the Party came down hard on the victim. For me it was the last straw.

My future lay elsewhere. The idea of quitting Cuba for good and travelling abroad became an obsession. Cuba was a prison island for me. I had become quite well-off since discovering Jose's infidelities and I could travel in comfort.

One day I received an encrypted message from someone claiming to be a colleague of the American agent I later learned was named Frank Reynolds. It scared the shit out of me. Was this really a CIA agent or had Cuban intelligence discovered me? The man tried to explain that Frank had suffered a personal tragedy, that he had abruptly quit the CIA and disappeared. He was totally off the grid. I pretended to go along and asked him to arrange for me to get out of the country so we could meet. Within days an invitation to speak about Havana's historical renovations in Paris at the *Ecole Speciale d'Architecture* arrived for me at work. I told my girls what I had been told had happened to Frank and suggested that we stop communicating until things settled down and I could learn more. I didn't tell them I wouldn't be coming back, in case one of them was the source of our betrayal. We could pick up the business again later, even if I were abroad. Leaving for Paris, I was delirious with excitement and I was scared to death.

Chapter 7

"You must be hungry, Ilan," Frank said. "Let me warm something up. I had no idea I'd talk this much. I've said more in the past few hours than I have the last ten years." He paused for a moment. "It does feel good, though, to have someone to talk with. If it gets too late for you to drive over the hill, you could bunk here and we can continue in the morning."

Ilan stood on the deck and stretched his arms over his head. A giant prehistoric-looking bird went lumbering by following the river downstream. "What's that?" he asked.

"That's Sylvia, our resident blue heron. She's ungainly, but very beautiful, I think. She lives in an old snag not far from here."

They went inside and Frank pulled a casserole out of the freezer and put it in the oven at a low temperature to thaw. "I don't trust these microwaves," he said.

Ilan looked around the house. Knowing Frank was pretty hard of hearing, he raised his voice from the living room. "Sounds like Celia saw your wife as a symbol for all she lost. Did she ever get to meet her, your wife?"

Frank didn't answer. He turned and walked out to the deck again and stared down at the river, his hands gripping the railing. He stayed like that for some time. Ilan could tell something was wrong, so he didn't follow. He sat on a stool and poured himself a glass of ice tea. Finally, Frank came back in.

"No," he said. "Joanna died shortly after this new arrangement with Celia started."

Ilan saw the hurt in Frank's eyes. The color of his skin changed and the tension on his face showed his age. The blood seemed to drain out of him. The whole room was charged with sadness. "I'm sorry," Ilan offered.

Frank walked over to a cabinet and took out a bottle of wine, then poured them each a glass and sat down. To his surprise, Frank began to tell the story. "I've only talked about this a couple of times. I think I've come to terms with it, but it's not something you ever get over. It's something to honor. But I'm surprised it still packs so much power for me." He paused for a minute collecting his thoughts, trying to decide where to start.

"While I was handling Celia, my real day job was to map the network of corruption that linked President Putin and the siloviki that ruled Russia with organized crime around the world. Russia's basically a mafia state, a criminal enterprise with nukes. Networks of corruption spread everywhere. I began uncovering thefts of state funds in countries from Malaysia to Argentina linked to Putin's FSB, the successor of the KGB. You wouldn't believe the scale of these schemes. When the Soviet Union fell apart, the former secret police in many of the

Communist countries were the only organized groups and they quickly filled the political vacuum that came in its wake. Muscle men with gold chains became the new kingpins behind some of the most corrupt regimes on earth. Neo-fascist Serbian gangs made links with South American drug lords. African rulers stole with impunity. Heroin moved from Asia to Europe under the protection of Romanian mafia. Ruling parties began stealing from their own sovereign wealth funds. It was a real ring of whores."

He looked up at Ilan, who stood transfixed. "I made many enemies, as you can imagine. Normally mobsters leave intelligence agencies alone. They do their thing and we do ours. We turn a blind eye most of the time in exchange for valuable information. But I was getting too close for comfort to exposures that could strip away the veneer of legitimacy that these mafia governments exploited. I was in Cartagena on a rare vacation with my wife Joanna, who had just retired from the CIA after thirty-five years. It was kind of a retirement party."

Frank wasn't sure he could tell this part without losing it. He was surprised how hard this was. Perhaps he had been too glib about 'honoring' the pain. It still hurt. Telling it out loud brought it all back. His hands trembled and he felt his throat contract. This was the calamity that ruined his life, which caused him to quit the Agency abruptly and leave civilization. He hadn't spoken of it to anyone for what, ten years?

"We had rented a car. I was supposed to pick up a friend at the airport who was joining us for the celebration, but Joanna said she'd drive while I finished the coffee she had poured me. I should have stopped her. I knew better. I knew, even before I heard the ignition, that I should have gone myself. I was already out of my chair when the blast blew the car and Joanna twenty feet in the air, killing her instantly. A blessing I guess. It killed me, too."

Chapter 8

It wasn't until I passed through security and took my seat that my heart stopped racing. When the plane finally lifted off the ground I let out an audible sigh of relief. I felt like I had just barely escaped. I wouldn't be using my return trip ticket and wondered whether I ever would be able to return to my homeland. Growing up a daughter of the revolution, the thought that I would ever live in exile was almost unimaginable. What would I tell Jose? How would I justify my actions to my father and mother? That I no longer believed their lies? Should I expose Jose's corruption and affairs to a wide audience? He deserved that. He deserved to be brought down. But the whole regime had rotted with power and privilege. The beautiful ideology of my youth had turned into empty slogans.

Dear Mom and Dad,

It is with a broken heart that I must tell you that I will not be coming home. I can no longer live with the hypocrisy around me. Jose can fill you in about all the prostitutes he hires and the drugs he uses with them. He can tell you how he pays for all this with his "commissions" from Swiss Immobilier. I know many other things about Jose (and you) that I'd rather not recount here. Instead, I've chosen to start a new life. I hope someday we can see each other again. I will always love you. Thank you for all that you have given me.

Celia

As soon as I finished writing this I began to cry. I buried my head in my hands and sobbed uncontrollably. The poor man in the seat next to me pretended not to notice. A stewardess kindly asked if she could help. I shook my head. The anxiety, the anger and the tension of the past months came to a climax, convulsing me. I walked to the back of the plane. Mercifully, the bathroom was vacant. I stayed in there a long time. I felt so much bitterness. Everything that I had ever held sacred had been taken from me. By the time I stopped crying I felt like an empty shell. But I had survived. You could even say I had triumphed. But it sure didn't feel like a victory; maybe more like redemption.

I had always wanted to travel. I'd be in Paris in a couple hours. The emptiness slowly gave way to the excitement of discovery. Soon I was in a taxi headed to my hotel. It felt like a slow-motion dream, a magical leap from the many films I had seen to the reality that is Paris. It was evening when I arrived. I checked into the hotel and went walking along the Seine by Notre Dame and the Louvre. Lights came on illuminating the monuments. My happiness started to return. I felt like singing or dancing. How romantic Paris was!

Later that evening I met Michael Steinmeyer in my hotel room, as we had arranged. I could tell immediately he was just another bland bureaucrat like so many I'd known in Cuba. Short, mostly bald, with psoriasis on his neck and face, he seemed nervous to meet me. I suspect it had more to do with my being a woman than the nature of our business. When I asked him whether the room was bugged, he said emphatically that it was not. I knew he was lying. No matter, this was all about business.

I was anxious to learn what had happened to Frank. Joe was reluctant to say much, only that there had been some kind of accident and his wife had been killed. Frank had disappeared, he said, but was not harmed. Not physically anyway. I learned later from other CIA agents I befriended that Frank had retreated to some land in northern California, "gone native," in the words of one of them. For some reason Frank's loss hurt more than my own. Perhaps I idealized the life he had with his wife, but I had placed what little hope I had for the possibility of true love in their relationship. His devotion to her was like a diamond in the ashes of my own marriage.

Michael tried his best to convince me to return to Cuba, but my decision was final. Later I went down to the lobby and posted the letter to my parents. It was done. "Les jeux sont fait." The business in Cuba could be started up again without my being there. Rita could handle it. I was free to do as I pleased. The money that the CIA had promised was safely in the accounts they had set up for me. The sums didn't seem real. I withdrew a large amount in cash from an ATM machine to reassure myself. The freedom to do as I wished was exhilarating. I stopped by an expensive boutique along the Rue St. Honore and bought an absurdly priced scarf. I had been so caught up in my fears about leaving that I hadn't given any real thought to what I would do after I got here.

I rented a furnished, ground floor apartment next to a salon du thé in the 11th arrondissement from a woman I met in the metro. She had come up to me in a state of some anxiety. "Mademoiselle," she said, "Il y a un homme completement a poile dans le metro." At first, I didn't understand her French, but she switched to fluent Spanish. "Miss, there's a man completely naked in the metro." At that moment a man appeared on the other end of the platform without a stitch of clothes."

A loudspeaker suddenly announced that the station was closing. She took my arm and told me she was carrying a considerable amount of cash with her and asked if I would kindly walk her to her apartment. It was on the Rue Chaligny off the Rue du Faubourg St. Antoine, walking distance from the Bastille. As we strode arm-in-arm through the streets of Paris, Marie explained that she bought and sold antique heirloom jewelry, travelling back and forth every three months between Paris and Buenos Aires. She said I could stay in her flat for three hundred dollars a month, if I wanted. It was perfect. I needed the time to sort things out in my life, plan my future.

Slowly the fear that I would somehow get arrested melted away and I began to relax into the enchantment of Paris. I got a copy of Victor Hugo's *Les Miserables*, my favorite book growing up, and brushed up on my French that way. Many of the streets where Inspector Javert chases Jean Valjean are the ones I walked on each day. I read most mornings on a bench across from Hugo's house on the Place des Vosges, surrounded by pigeons and young harried mothers and their well-behaved children. A part of me was drawn to Hugo's revolutionary romanticism. I guess I couldn't completely rid myself of it. I think it was a way to stay emotionally connected to my family. But another part of me was in grief. I had left everything I once loved and was all alone in a foreign country. Marie had a collection of old Spanish blues albums on vinyl. I'd listen to them over and over and cry each evening. My thoughts, though, returned to Frank and his wife. I couldn't get them out of my mind. I kept imagining the suffering he was feeling. It tormented me. Finally, I decided to fly to California to try to find him. It was crazy, I realized. Michael, or whatever his real name was, told me that even the CIA didn't know where he was; but he helped me get a visa anyway. The day Marie returned from Argentina, I flew to San Francisco. I knew exactly where I'd find him.

Chapter 9

The silence was awkward. Finally, Ilan reached over and placed his hand over Frank's clenched fist. Their eyes met.

Frank nodded. "It was hard," he acknowledged. He filled Ilan's glass and then his own.

Ilan raised his for a toast. "To Joanna."

They touched glasses. Frank sighed, relieved to get the story out. He was not used to such intimacy. Simba looked up at him, attuned to his emotions. Frank drained his glass and poured himself another.

Ilan felt humbled by Frank's unguarded vulnerability. In the silence he heard the river. It surprised him that he hadn't noticed the sound before. It was as if the space around them had come back into focus. He had been there and now he was here again. "What did you do after that?" Ilan asked, breaking the spell.

"I was desperate, insane with grief and anger," Frank answered, fortified by the wine. "I knew my life was over. Joanna and I were totally fused. We were one. We shared our every experience. We couldn't stand being apart." He sighed again.

"I tried so hard to keep the connection. It felt like she was in the room with me. I talked to her constantly." He smiled. "I still do."

He paused. "I thought a lot about killing myself. The pain was just too great and I saw no way to go on. I also thought a lot about revenge, but it was me they were after, not her. It was my fault. In any case, who would I get my revenge against? The person who set the bomb? The one who ordered it? The whole rotten system? I wondered what it would have been like, if I had been the one killed. I wouldn't have wanted her to experience what I felt. Better she went first."

"Eventually, I returned to Washington. I met with the honchos in the 'Company.' They were very kind. My closest friend, Howie, flew to DC and offered to let me stay on his land. I agreed to work as his caretaker in return, though I didn't know the first thing about that. I told my bosses that I had to resign and made them promise not to contact me again. I went through the obligatory debrief and exit interview, signed all their forms and flew to California."

"Did they keep their promise? Did anyone ever contact you?" Ilan asked.

"No, they were good about that. Celia was the only one to find me."

Ilan looked up, surprised, "Celia?"

"Yes, she had gone to Paris to meet with another agent who replaced me as her handler. She defected, lived in Paris for a while. The news of my wife's killing really rattled her. She wanted to comfort me. I think she also needed me to help her make sense of her life and figure out what to do with it. It's ironic because I was probably the last person on earth to advise someone about that. For me, the future no longer existed. In a way, though, we both needed to reinvent ourselves. But we were headed in opposite directions. My only desire was to retreat back to nature, to 'compost myself,' as I liked to tell her. She wanted to discover the world, to engage with it. She was fascinated by modernity with all its gadgets, with the ability to travel and communicate. She told me it was like being a blind person all her life and suddenly she could see."

"How did she find you here?" asked Ilan.

"That was funny," Frank responded. "No one knew where I had gone, except Howie and his wife. Actually, I don't think the agency could have found me, even if it tried. But Celia had once asked me what Joanna and I dreamed of doing after we both retired and I mentioned this land. She never forgets a thing. She flew to San Francisco, rented a car and drove up here. I thought I was in 'deep cover,' as we used to say; but she showed up here one day in a rented red convertible. It blew me away."

Ilan shook his head. "I suppose it would."

"I pretended to be angry. In fact, I was glad to have someone to talk to. Celia's a great listener. It's a real talent. She draws people out. We spent hours each day walking and talking. Sometimes when I cried she would hold me. We talked about her feelings as a defector. Her parents were furious with her. They felt greatly betrayed. They all but disowned her. Jose never even wrote back. He was probably afraid of what else she might expose. After a week or so like that, in a kind of perpetual co-therapy, we began to process the past less and less. Instead, we argued."

Chapter 10

"Welcome to San Francisco," the immigration officer said, greeting me with a smile as he handed me back my landing card. Whatever visa Michael had gotten me worked like a Get-Out-of-Jail-Free card. I couldn't believe how easy it was to enter the city of my dreams. I changed some money, hailed a cab and got dropped off at a Bed and Breakfast adjacent to Washington Square Park in North Beach, home of the beat-niks and hipsters I had once idolized. Like Paris, I had a good idea of what the city looked like from hours and hours of films and television shows. But being here was different.

I couldn't wait to see the sites. I had spent hours exploring the Internet alone in my apartment on the Rue Chaligny. I trolled through this vast virtual universe, which was so limited to me in Cuba. It was almost as exciting as being a tourist in the real world. By the time I got to San Francisco I was well prepared with a carefully planned itinerary on Google Maps. I loved walking past the mansions in Pacific Heights and through Golden Gate Park, felt most at home in the heart of the Mission, and especially enjoyed getting up early to watch the Chinese practice Tai Chi and Qigong in the park by my hotel. The city lived up to all my romantic dreams. But I was anxious to find Frank.

I rented a red Mustang convertible from Hertz. They took a frustrating half hour to approve my Cuban drivers' license, but I finally headed out of the city on a clear, windy day across the Golden Gate bridge north up Highway 101 with the top down blasting the radio. At Healdsburg the traffic finally started thinning out and in no time I was alone on the road surrounded by vineyards and lush rolling hills in the distance, singing along with a classic rock station on XM Radio. I could not have been happier. I wondered what I would say to Frank once I found him. Would he even agree to see me? I had already located Feather Mountain on the Carmella River from a few Google searches and had it plotted on my Navigator. I'd be there in four hours and twelve minutes, it told me.

I stopped for gas in a small town down the road from him. It was the end of summer and there was some smoke in the air from nearby forest fires. The sun had turned an unnatural orange that produced a slightly ominous feeling in my stomach. Along the road to Feather Mountain, I passed an organic farm with a large produce stand. I turned around in a cloud of dust and pulled up to it. *I shouldn't come empty handed*, I thought. There were white and yellow peaches, corn piled high in wheel barrows, flats of red tomatoes ready for canning and fields of "pick-em yourself" flowers. I bought more than I should have, probably, and walked along the rows of sunflowers, gladiolas, daisies, zinnias, snapdragons and scores of others whose names

I didn't know, cutting an enormous bouquet. I asked the farmer about Frank. He pointed up the road. "Just a mile as the crow flies," and his eyes followed me with curiosity as I walked back to my car with my arms filled with fruits and flowers.

I drove slowly down the steep gravel driveway to Frank's place with growing trepidation. Near the end of the road I stopped. My heart was beating fast. I was having last minute doubts. *Why am I being so presumptuous? I hardly know Frank. He obviously needed to escape from his past, from the world at large. Why would I violate that?* I thought. I heard a dog barking, growing louder. I wanted to turn around. I couldn't back up. I drove on, hoping I wouldn't encounter him. I knew I had made a mistake.

A man approached with his dog. I didn't know what to say or do. He came over to my side. He looked shocked. "Celia?" he asked. It was Frank. I simply didn't recognize him. He was bearded. His hair was white. He had aged twenty years.

"Frank?"

He looked confused, alarmed. I could see his mind spinning, trying to figure out what the fuck I was doing there. "What the hell are you doing here?" he asked. "How'd you find me?"

He was dumbfounded. I was embarrassed to my core. I stammered. "I'm so sorry. I shouldn't have come. When I heard about your tragedy, my heart broke for you. I thought you might need a friend, someone to talk to. I knew how close you were to your wife and…" I couldn't continue. All my words sounded false, stupid. I felt like a schoolgirl embarrassed at being caught in the men's bathroom or something. He just shook his head, his face in a scowl, looking somewhere between terrified and mentally unstable.

"Park over there," he said, pointing to the front of an old barn. I did and got out of my car. "I'm totally confused," he said. "Why are you here?"

I looked in his eyes and saw broken glass, a broken heart. The strong, confident Frank I had met in Mexico was shattered. In its place was an old man, his hair turned white overnight. He was dirty and weathered. I could hardly believe it was the same person. "Frank, I'm sorry. I knew when I came down your driveway that I shouldn't have come here. I'm intruding. Please forgive me. I remembered your saying it was your wife's and your dream to retire here, so I figured this is where you'd be. I left Paris and flew to San Francisco on a whim and drove up here. I just wanted to help you in any way I could."

He stared at me, not so much in anger as in disbelief. "Paris?" he asked.

I stuttered, hurrying to explain. "I defected," I told him. "When I received an encrypted message from some stranger claiming to be your replacement, I thought we had been discovered. This agent—he called himself Michael Steinmeyer—arranged for me to give a talk in Paris. I met him there. All he could tell me was that your wife had died in an accident and that you had quit your job and disappeared. I pressed him, but he said the even the agency didn't know where you were. But I remembered your talking about this place. I just wanted to reach out."

He looked at me and at the car with its bouquet on the passenger seat and the bag of fruit. "Well, it's too late for you to drive back," he said, glancing up at the sky. "You'll have to stay here." He didn't say I was welcome to. He seemed irritated, angry, exposed. He helped me with my bags and we walked to the big house. There were sprinklers turning like dervishes in an orchard heavy with fruit on our right. In front of the house was a lawn slopping down to the most magnificent trees I had ever seen, a row of virgin redwoods. We walked around to the front of the house and up some steps to a wide porch. "May I get you something to drink?" he asked.

I sat in a tall wicker chair. In a few minutes he came out carrying a tray with two glasses of water and a bowl with the peaches I brought cut into slices. He placed them on a table next to me and pulled up another chair. He sat quietly, not saying a word. I couldn't bear the silence.

"Please forgive me, Frank. I just didn't know any other way to contact you. I was hurting myself. I left everything behind in Cuba, my mother and father, my friends, my marriage, all my dreams. You were the only person I trusted, still believed in. Something, some belief in the future, was broken when I heard about the accident. I couldn't stop thinking about what unbearable suffering you must be going through. I had to do something."

There was a long, uncomfortable silence. Finally, Frank spoke. "It was no accident, Celia. Someone planted a bomb under my car, hoping to kill me. Got Joanna instead. I couldn't go on after that. It would have been easier if I had had the courage to kill myself then. But I didn't. Being here, surrounded by nature, has been good for me, though. It all makes some sense here in the bigger picture. And I have Simba," he said, petting the dog and smiling for the first time.

Coming to terms with a random accident would be hard enough, I thought, but a car bomb?

"How'd you get Simba?" I asked.

"Found him. Or, he found me. He just came to me the first morning I was here. No collar, nothing. I asked all around, left posters, but never heard from his owner. The local vet gave him a clean bill of health. After a couple of weeks, I stopped looking."

I let out a deep breath and looked around at the scenery. My heart slowly returned to normal. "It's beautiful. I can see why you came here."

Frank offered a slight smile. "It's very nurturing, helps to restore one's faith. I'm learning how to work with my hands. It feels a lot more honest than the life of deception I led before. The birds don't have secrets. The trees, if they have any, keep them to themselves. There's no one tapping my phones, if I had one. No people whose lives I put in danger. Plenty of fruit just hanging for me to pick. By the way, thanks for the peaches," he said.

I nodded. "So, tell me, Celia, what are your plans? Where are you living? How did your family respond when you defected? How are the girls you recruited?"

I told him everything. I had no idea what I was going to do, even what country I'd live in. The business in Cuba was shut down for the time being, though Rita was eager to start it up again. I was struggling whether to get my license and a job as an architect, probably in Paris or Spain, or just travel for a while or even to open my intelligence agency somewhere else. That idea wouldn't leave my mind. While I was driving, I couldn't stop thinking about it. I had a proven business model. Could I do that again in some other country? I asked Frank's advice.

"I hate that world. I've left it for good. I'd recommend you do the same: take what money you have and buy yourself an old cottage somewhere in the south of France and just live there. Take up gardening and painting. It's a good life. Honest. Rewarding. But you're young and ambitious. You'd probably get bored," he said.

"Do you ever get bored here?" I asked.

"I haven't been bored for one moment. Everything around me is so interesting. I read. I learn how to fix things. I cook for myself. I swim during the day and watch the stars at night. It's anything but boring."

I smiled. "It must be painful, though, being here without her. It was your dream."

His face twitched. He shut his eyes. "It's an unfillable void, an emptiness that terrified me at first. I'm learning to live with it, though. I pray to it. It's hardest at night. I look up at the stars and we talk to each other. She still feels very near. We were really one. I guess she still lives inside me. She would be happy I'm here."

Chapter 11

I planned to leave the next morning, but I ended up remaining almost three months. Frank was very gracious. It was Frank who insisted I stay that morning after serving me a breakfast of pancakes and yogurt. He said that as long as I was here, I should take advantage of experiencing the redemptive power of nature, "how forgiving it was," as he said. I knew he resented my intruding on him, so I left him mostly to himself. I could see that he got something out of taking care of me, though. He was very protective, a "giver" personality. It was kind of ironic since I came there to help him. But he loved cooking for me and sharing what he had learned. He loved his solitude more, though. I respected that and gave him his space.

I spent the days in the big house on Jennifer's computer and Wi-Fi. Frank wouldn't go near it. I couldn't get enough of the Internet. I was addicted. In the late afternoons, though, I would walk to the river and swim. Frank showed me how you could float up and down the river on a plastic blow-up air mattress, the kind you usually see in swimming pools. On especially hot days, we would lie on them on our backs and use our arms to paddle headfirst upstream. If you caught the eddies just right, depending on the direction of the wind, you wouldn't even have to paddle. Frank called it "floating upriver." It was the metaphor for how he wanted to live his life. I must admit that suspended on the air mattress, carried effortlessly upstream against the current, gave me a profound sense of peace, a kind of meditation of the body. Often, the float back was so slow as to be almost imperceptible. Time stopped.

Frank's connection to nature was beautiful to observe. It had become his religion and I saw him change while I was here. The rapture he felt seemed to heal his wounds a bit. He began to put on weight, though there remained not an ounce of fat on him. His posture changed. His gait became light. He even let me cut his hair. We'd often have dinner together at night. He loved to tell me his views about the mind of nature, how natural selection was the essence of intelligence—in our brains, in nature and the universe as a whole. He was in awe of it. But these epiphanies could only take him so far. The pain of the loss of his wife had become a defining part of him. It left a hole that couldn't be filled. He had permanently withdrawn from the world.

As the days turned into weeks and months, I realized I was falling in love with this man. I tried not to. He could never reciprocate. I completely honored his loss. No one could replace the love he had for Joanna. I realized, however, that this restriction in our relationship, which I respected, only added to the passion I felt for him. But I never let him see what I was feeling. I don't know if he could tell. He never let on, if he did. We grew closer, but never physically so. I think he saw me as his student. It probably would have surprised him to know that I was attracted to him. He was twice my age.

We were also moving in opposite directions. I was looking for my place in the world. He was retreating from it. I loved all that technology and modernity had to offer. He despised it. He thought it was the heart of our problems. In Frank's eyes I was wasting my life sitting all day in front of a computer screen while outside, surrounding me, was the glory of nature. Everything I needed to learn about life, he insisted, every insight into the nature of being and existence, was there for the taking, right before my eyes, if only I'd look. We argued all the time, but lovingly, never to hurt each other.

I countered that we had a moral obligation to engage with the world, a duty to ease suffering, to make the world a better place. He would say that this was a selfish delusion, an ego thing. "Get your self out of the way," he would say, "and see if there's still a problem. The world is perfect as it is." I argued that he was the one being selfish. He was given this free ride in paradise. He was spoiled. The world could use his help. It already had. Wasn't it a good thing that he had saved the lives of those agents in Tehran? What if he could prevent a war? He found that funny. "There will always be wars," he laughed. "There will always be the next thing to stop." Maybe what the world really needed was for more people to disengage from it, like he was doing, he suggested.

Many nights he spent alone in his little shack with his boats or reading. Sometimes he would write, but he never shared any of that with me. During the day he took care of the orchard and the road and cut the grass in front of the house. I teased him that he should be doing it by hand instead of using the riding lawn mower. When the tractor or the truck broke down, I showed him how to fix it. I was from Cuba, after all. He liked that I knew how things worked. I showed him how to improve his garden and what he could plant for the coming winter. I helped him fix the water system, which seemed to have problems every week or so. He taught me tai chi, which I had been dying to learn. Sometimes we would read to each other, mostly classics. It was a loving, satisfying relationship in almost every way. But I knew I had to get on with my life. There was no future with Frank and I was too young not to have a future. Plus, Frank began to insist that I stop talking about engaging with the world and actually do it. He was my biggest supporter. He wanted me to succeed with whatever I wanted, even if it were the opposite of what he would have chosen for me.

I began to get increasingly serious about setting up a private intelligence agency with prostitutes, as I had done in Cuba. It was either that or settle down somewhere and get my architecture license. I went back and forth in my mind, but I knew I had become addicted to the rush of undercover work. The risks were exciting, the return on investment astronomical and the sense of empowerment was a real turn-on. I studied the Internet for places that would be a good market for the secrets I hoped to gather. I began to focus on Abu Dhabi, the federal capital and center of government in the United Arab

Emirates and one of the most modern cities in the world. Ostentatious wealth was everywhere. Abu Dhabi had a reputation as the premier sex tourism destination in the Middle East. The rich and privileged prayed in the Gulf, it is said, but fucked in Abu Dhabi. And what better place for political intrigue than the heart of the Arab world?

Part Two

Chapter 12

Seven miles and seven minutes past the site of the ambush, the black van turned off the Sarghoda-Faisalabad Highway and drove on hard, dry clay another two miles before pulling into a garage by an old farm house. A hydraulic lift lowered the van below ground level, the opening above it then covered with a steel plate and a stack of old rugs. The driver and one guard hugged the four men who were waiting for them. They were excited, but remained calm. These were all grown men who had fought continuously since they were old enough to hold a rifle. Their discipline and strength were palpable, bodies erect, eyes that had seen many deaths. They had beaten the Soviet Army, fought the Americans to a stalemate and now, with this bomb, they were prepared to take on the world. The operation had gone off with military precision. The intelligence was spot-on, none of their mujahideen had even been scratched and they left fifteen of their enemy dead. The motorcyclists were long gone in the opposite direction. Now they would drink tea, pray and wait.

David Hoffman

In capitals around the world presidents conferred with their generals to track events and authorized the counter-terrorism and nuclear weapons extraction plans they had hoped never to need. It was their ultimate nightmare, a loose nuke in the hands of a rogue terrorist organization, yet to be identified.

The U.S. President got off the phone with his Pakistani counterpart and held his head in his hands. "Nothing," he said to the security chiefs standing in front of his desk in the Oval Office. "They are completely stonewalling. He says that, despite the rumors, he has been assured that all their nuclear weapons have been accounted for." He turned to his National Security Advisor. "You'd better get over there as quickly as possible."

Geo-stationary satellites shifted into position over the site of the attack. Armed Predator drones flew overhead despite the Pakistan Airforce's warning it would shoot down any unauthorized aircraft. Pictures began to fill the screens in the White House Situation Room where the security chiefs reconvened. On the monitors were four charred vehicles, a total of fifteen bodies marked with fluorescent green arrows, six ambulances and a satellite TV uplink truck. And images began to show the carnage on millions of Pakistani television sets as well, as Geo TV broadcast live from the scene. Soon these pictures streamed around the world.

Tweets from motorists who were backed up on the freeway described the green lorry ploughing into the lead car, the hordes of motorcyclists, the frenzy of automatic weapons fire, the white van exploding and the bloody aftermath. News spread quickly on social media. Less than a half hour after the ambush, Pakistan's Chief of the Army told a hastily arranged news conference that there was absolutely no truth to the rumors that a nuclear weapon was stolen. "I state categorically that no nuclear weapons are missing. Our arsenal remains 100% secure."

But India's Research and Analysis Wing, its primary foreign intelligence agency, was not reassured. They noted the unprecedented mobilization of all sectors of Pakistani security, the unusual press conference and, most ominously, the deployment of highly sensitive radiological detection equipment with Pakistan's elite counter-insurgency forces. If an atomic bomb had indeed been captured, India was the most likely destination. Security was tightened along the border and every effort made to find out what had actually happened.

A sense of panic began to spread. But the Pakistanis, despite intense pressure from India, China, Russia and the U.S., would not budge. "All of our strategic weapons are safe and fully accounted for," the indomitable spokesman for the National Control Authority repeated ad nauseum. There had been previous attacks on military bases that had raised alarms about the safety of Pakistan's nukes—one that breached the security perimeter at the Kamra air base, and a threat to assault the nuclear complex at Dera Ghazi Khan—but nothing had turned up the heat like this. "This, too, will pass," he assured everyone.

In the farm house near Faisalabad the mujahideen sipped tea and smoked hashish from a nargila, recounting war stories. In Israel Chaim Ratner called his close friend General Rashid, whose mother was recuperating from an operation in a Tel Aviv hospital, for information. Indian and Afghan agents worked feverishly with their contacts inside Pakistan's security apparatus. Chinese technicians who helped maintain the missiles at the Sarghoda airbase reported to Beijing what they were learning on the ground. Slowly, a picture developed from thousands of intercepts and informants that contradicted the government's line.

A consensus began to emerge that, indeed, a small tactical nuclear weapon, which had been secretly developed to fit atop the M-11 missile, had been lost. Weighing just under a hundred pounds, the bomb could be dropped from a plane or smuggled inside a car or even carried across the mountains in a backpack. The yield was likely no more than 50 kilotons, relatively puny by nuclear standards, but enough to destroy a small city. The biggest unanswered question was whether the weapon had been mated or not. For security purposes the radioactive core was usually kept separate from the trigger mechanism and a two-person control system was necessary to unlock the permissive action links. But in practice, some analysts claimed that fully-mated bombs were routinely rotated between bases as this one, apparently, had been. There was absolutely no word yet on who the perpetrators might be, but there were plenty of candidates.

Chapter 13

Simba started barking and rushed out of the house. "Probably bears," said Frank. He and Ilan walked out to the orchard to see. It was a beautiful evening, an almost full moon rising over the hill behind them. By the time they got to the action Simba had treed a bear which clung to the trunk of an old apple tree in awkward embarrassment. "He does a good job chasing them away. They pull down the branches and can do a lot of damage, but Simba terrifies them."

Both men were quiet as they walked back to the house. They had been at it for hours and were tired. It felt like they were deep underwater, buffeted by the tides. "How 'bout we change the subject for a while? Frank said. "Tell me about yourself. On second thought, let me show you where you can sleep and we can continue this tomorrow."

The next morning Frank was up early. He had slept poorly but was anxious to get back to his story. It surprised him how much he liked telling it, however painful it could be. He wasn't used to hearing his voice so much, though he sometimes talked out loud to himself or Simba. The stellar jays were

screeching and the sun was just peaking above the hills on the opposite side of the river when Ilan woke up.

Ilan was also excited to get started. He had had the best sleep in years. The interview was going better than he could have wished. He was eager to get to the Abraham plot, though. Frank's story, he realized, could make a book in itself. He poured himself some coffee and filled a bowl with granola, huckleberries and goat milk. "Do you eat this well every morning?" he asked.

Frank smiled.

Ilan took out a Kindle to read the morning's news and asked Frank for the password to the Wi-fi.

"Haven't got a clue. But I think there may be instructions taped to the back of that cabinet by the refrigerator," he said pointing.

Ilan downloaded several newspapers as Frank ate quietly. "You don't follow the news anymore?" he asked Frank.

"Less and less," admitted Frank. "Celia would get it on her computer and sometimes we'd listen to an NPR podcast. But one day we listened for quite a while, all about the fighting in one country or another. Finally, something was said that made us realize it was an old podcast. Turned out it was two years old! But even Celia, who studied the news like a scientist, didn't realize it was old news for a good ten minutes. It was just the same story, endlessly going 'round and 'round. Nothing really changes."

"You're not much into technology, I take it," Ilan asked.

"No. Celia and I argued endlessly about that, too. I think machines should be extensions of people, not the other way around. But people like her were becoming extensions of their machines. She was addicted to the screen. I really couldn't understand it, not when we were surrounded by this infinitely fascinating natural world. My goal was to have a direct perception of this reality. All these gadgets just got in the way. I didn't want any mediation. I wanted to take it in directly with all my senses." He paused, realizing he was sounding too agitated about it. "I don't like the modern world. Cities are abominations to me, covering over all living things with cement and urban sprawl. We're breeding way too many people who are rushing to these cities putting more pressure on our planet than it can handle." He stopped. He didn't want to sound like some eco-terrorist.

Ilan brought out his recorder. There was a raucous of bird sounds from the deck. When it quieted Ilan gestured to the recorder and Frank nodded his approval.

Ilan asked, "What else did you and Celia argue about?"

"Mostly about what to do with our lives," Frank said, as he called Simba back. "It was very good natured, mind you. She thought my monastic life should be a temporary respite from the world, a time and place for me to recover. But after that, I should re-engage, not necessarily in the same line of work. She thinks we all have an obligation to improve the lot of others. She called me a 'born-again survivalist.' I told her that she was still afflicted with the illusions of her revolutionary Communist upbringing."

"Did she ever tempt you?" asked Ilan.

"To leave here?" laughed Frank. "Not a chance. I told her it would take a nuclear bomb to force me from here."

"This doesn't seem the place for an architect, organizer of prostitutes, spy and defector," Ilan said. "How long did she stay?"

"A couple of months," said Frank thinking. "Maybe three."

"I'm surprised," said Ilan. "You two sound like the odd couple."

"No, we actually got along great. She loved it here, loved the river and the birds. I left her alone most days, left her in her virtual world. She liked solitude as much as I did. Some people need to be around other people. Not Celia. She thrived in the silence here. We'd meet most nights and cook together. We didn't speak much. We didn't need to. We got very close. It was like we always knew what the other was thinking. She'd say something and I'd already be thinking it and vice versa. We'd read to each other. When the moon was bright, we'd sometimes go down and swim in the river."

"She had a beautiful body. I never let her see me notice her, see how attracted I was to her. For one thing, I thought I was too old for her. I once listened to a review of a James Bond movie on the radio and the woman said that it made her ill when Sean Connery kissed his young co-star. The 'ick factor,' she called it. And that was Sean Connery! I was afraid Celia would think it was pervy, if she knew I fantasized about her. Of course, I wasn't ready for her, either. I wasn't ready for anyone. It was just a couple of years after Joanna died when

Celia showed up. I was still deeply mourning her. There was no room for someone else."

"But it sounds like you and Celia got so much from each other," Ilan reflected.

"Oh, we did. I knew I was growing attached to her, despite myself. I resisted it every day. I had an on-going conversation with Joanna about it in my head. She thought I should go for it. But I wouldn't dare. I really wasn't ready. Being around Celia every day, though, made me admire her more and more. She cared about people. She'd do anything for me, more than anyone, even Joanna, if I were really being honest with myself. She was a real pleaser personality. She was very protective, like a mother bear. And she was smart, too. I loved talking philosophy and metaphysics with her. She was actually quite a talented painter, too. I have several of her paintings in my little cave, if you want to see them. She would spend long afternoons when the harsh glare of the sun dimmed or in the early morning light out in the orchard or on the bluff overlooking the river with paints and an easel she had delivered here, happy as could be. I learned to love the peace and solitude that surrounded her then. She was more beautiful even than the outdoors she painted. It was such a contrast to the woman frantically typing on her computer. I used to wish I could just freeze time when I saw her so perfectly contented standing by her easel. She looked like an angel."

They were silent for some time. Frank couldn't believe how he opened up with this man.

"What made her leave?" asked Ilan finally.

Frank thought for a while. "I pushed her out, I guess. She needed a real life, not caretaking a hermit in mourning. She deserved to love someone, to find her soul mate, as I had done with Joanna. She kept obsessing about starting up her business again, somewhere else. She was convinced she could do it in Abu Dhabi with its intersection of geo-political ambitions, oil wealth, terrorism and prostitutes. I encouraged her. She thanked me for letting her stay for so long and promised not to interrupt my precious solitude anymore. She gave me a cell phone as a gift, just for the two of us. She said we could only call each other, if it were a matter of life and death. Her leaving was a huge loss for me. Having just begun to finally heal from Joanna's death, I faced losing Celia. It was only when she drove away up the driveway that I could really admit to myself how I had fallen in love again."

Chapter 14

Leaving Frank's driveway, I felt a sense of loss like I had never felt before, even worse than leaving my family behind in Cuba. I pulled off the road and cried in waves of grief. My stomach felt like the bottom of the ocean. I considered turning around and going back, but Frank had been pretty adamant that it was time for me to go. I had spent almost three months there, completely uninvited. I knew he didn't want me to leave for his own sake, though. He enjoyed having me around, but he thought it was best for me. He was probably right. I had to get on with my life.

I moved to Abu Dhabi where there was no shortage of political intrigue and valuable, well-guarded secrets. Prostitution was ubiquitous, if technically illegal. The girls came from the former Soviet Union, from China and South East Asia, from Brazil, Germany and every other part of the world. Prices could be twice what it cost to hire a woman in Europe. It was a playground for the rich and powerful.

Although my personal bank account was flush, I knew I would need start-up capital. I contacted Michael Steinmeyer,

Frank's replacement at the CIA, told him my plans and asked for a loan. I promised to give the CIA first right of refusal for any information I gleaned, but I would not be exclusive. I'd sell to any government. Like the girls I planned to hire, any customer with money would do. Everything was transactional. I would make my company available for special assignments, if he had particular requests. He said he'd get back to me. It didn't take long. I was provided a CIA contact at the embassy, given a line of credit for $100,000 and told that, depending on the quality of information I uncovered, more funds could be forthcoming.

The new agent gave me plenty of advice, including the specific hotels where individuals of interest were likely to stay. With his help, it didn't take long for me to get the lay of the land. I even considered starting my own high-end brothel, but I knew I'd be over my head. I learned what any man visiting Abu Dhabi for the first time might learn. Compared to other cities, there was little sex advertising online. It was all done by word of mouth. Hotel managers and even baggage boys knew where to score. I paid them handsomely for information. Within a few months I gained advance notice of who was coming to town, who were the players and what girls and agencies serviced them. The girls I talked to were suspicious at first. I had to be discreet about my past experiences, but I soon won their trust with generous bonuses for signing up with me.

I loved my girls. I felt like a madam. I was overly cautious and protective. At first the information they provided was pretty pedestrian, intimate profiles on a number of important political and business figures, pending mergers and acquisitions, things like that. But I continued to pay them well and slowly trained them how to coax the kinds of information that would bring in top dollars. My big break happened when Irina, a vivacious blond from Estonia who looked like she had just walked off a fashion show runway in Paris, escorted a gunrunner from Russia who was meeting with a shadowy sheik from Qatar. My contact was excited with this catch and Irina managed to accompany the Russian for three nights of cocaine-filled orgies with three friends she brought along. With that one score, I was able to pay Michael back much of the initial loan. I also adroitly sold the same information to the Israelis, Saudis and Australians. The girls played the ground game. My job was to establish contacts with different intelligence agencies, which were eager to buy what I had to sell. In Cuba, we had operated as a co-op; but now I acted as the sole proprietor. I was more than generous, however.

I began getting special requests. Through my network of hotel informants, it was easy to steer the right girls to specific targets of great interest. My CIA contact at the embassy repeatedly asked me to have the girls wired, but I refused. I didn't want them to take the risk. The way we worked, there was nothing they were doing that could be traced to any intelligence operations. What they told me was all done discreetly in places where we couldn't be recorded. Nothing was written down. In a similar way, I exchanged their information with my spy friends who deposited funds in well-camouflaged accounts. I assumed all the risks. The girls had little to lose.

Everything went exceedingly well for a year. I had trouble keeping up with all the requests. But I began to fear we were getting too big, exactly what I had feared in Cuba. "The only thing we have to fear is success itself," Frank used to tell me. Then one day a bombshell fell in our laps.

Chapter 15

Paola Vasquez worked the bar like she usually did at Happy Hour. She loved the hors d'oeuvres and the bartenders knew to keep her drinks extra light. No one bothered her, not anymore, not since Celia hired some female vets from Craig's list, ex-U.S. Army Special Forces, to mess with the pimps who thought they had a monopoly at the Jumeirah at Etihad Towers. Paola's escort agency hadn't been willing to protect her, but the pimps and their enforcers were no match for Celia's amazons.

The Jumeirah was considered the most expensive hotel in the world and prostitutes there could command fees of $5000 and up. The hotel management was happy to have Celia run the pimps out of there and the night managers enjoyed the generous commissions she paid them. She even worked out a deal to rent an apartment in the hotel at a great discount. Word of her support for Paola gave her street creds that won her the respect and trust of the other girls she recruited.

Paola was her favorite. She was the center of attention in whatever room she entered. She was of average height but with luxurious coffee-colored hair, doe-like chocolate eyes and a

David Hoffman

body that would have made Botticelli weep. As one Saudi prince ironically commented, she caused one to "believe in god." She was smart, too, which made her a quick study in the art of intelligence seduction.

Relatively well-off now, she had grown up in one of the poorest favelas in Sao Paolo, for which she was named. One evening, largely on a dare and a bit drunk, she offered herself to a businessman she noticed coming out of a luxury hotel. He was cute and obviously rich, an Italian it turned out, and he obligingly took her up on her offer. The cash he gave her was more money than she had ever seen before. She gave it to her alcoholic mother, told her she had found it on a street outside that hotel. The mother looked at her with knowing eyes, but didn't say a word. Paola had discovered a way to turn her astounding beauty into wealth and a ticket out of the slums. She was fifteen.

She noticed the tall, dark haired man staring at her from the other end of the bar. She could have her choice of men. She liked the looks of him, the cut of his expensive suit, the way he held himself. She could tell in an instant he was a man of substance. She quickly looked him up and down, then turned back to her drink and the wasabi sirloin steak hors d'oeuvres that were her favorite. He would come to her, she knew.

"May I join you?" he asked. She gave him that practiced seductive smile that said she was available for the right price. He sat next to her. His accent was South Asian, Pakistani perhaps. He had the eyelashes for sure. A gold Rolex watch hung below his cuffed shirt sleeve. He told her he was a Saudi,

94

a black sheep from one of the royal families. He lived mostly in Lahore, but travelled a great deal. It didn't take long for him to ask and for her to answer. He paid for their drinks, left a large tip, and escorted her to his room on the 56th floor.

She could size men up in an instant. If they had good eye contact, they would not be violent or too kooky. If they wore the right cologne, they would be clean. Too much and they were not. If they did not try to kiss her immediately when they were alone in the elevator, they were more likely to be good lovers. When she did finally kiss him, she knew she had found a man experienced at pleasing a woman. He called himself Hassan Al Kidwa, the name he used when he checked in, as she discovered later. It was men like this, fairly rare in her experience, that made her job seem almost too good to be true. She stepped back, a little breathlessly—not completely an act—held a finger to her lips and called the agency to tell them she was alright and the room number. He counted out 50 one hundred-dollar bills from a stack he kept in the inside pocket of his suit coat and handed them to her.

After ordering two bottles of champagne, he took out a mirror that already had many lines of cocaine neatly arranged in long rows from a bedside table. Clearly, he had planned for an evening like this. He took off his jacket and tie and kicked off his loafers. She took off the pearl earrings and necklace she wore and carefully unclasped the spaghetti straps on her 6-inch fuck me shoes. She liked how slowly he moved. He was in no hurry. This would be no quickie. The champagne arrived almost immediately.

The sex was phenomenal. He was confident enough in himself to let her lead much of the time. It was light and playful. When he came, he screamed with utter abandon. She pretended to join him, but she could have let herself go for real, she knew. They showered together, snorted more coke and started again. He was getting quite drunk from all the champagne. She had only sipped a taste.

The phone rang. He pushed her off him in a hurry and sprang to answer it. His demeanor changed. He spoke in a language she didn't understand, Urdu she assumed, but then switched to Arabic, which she did. Something had arrived, she overheard, something glorious, earthshaking. It would change the course of history. "Yes, there would be many martyrs," he said. "It couldn't be helped, but they will all go directly to heaven." He paid her no attention. His back was to her. He seemed to forget she was in the room.

"Yes, you mustn't move it too quickly. It will be too dangerous. Do as we planned. The Indians and the Americans and ISI will be everywhere within the hour. We must be patient. From now on we will communicate, as we agreed: no phones, only messengers you trust. Use the Gmail account, if you need to communicate more quickly, but do not send it. We both can access it; but if it is not sent, it cannot be intercepted. You understand? If there's a big problem on my end, I will place an ad in *The Dawn* as we agreed. Yes? Yes? Of course."

He turned and saw her get up and go to the bathroom, but she stayed just out of his sight and listened. "Let the temples of the infidels turn to dust." He was drunk on champagne and power. More laughter. He congratulated the man on the other end. "We will all go down in history," he said. "Insha'Allah." He looked at his watch. *Thirty days and twelve hours to go*, he thought.

As soon as she heard him saying good-bye, she moved to flush the toilet. Her heart was beating rapidly. She looked at herself in the mirror. She must not show any anxiety. When she came out, he said to her in Arabic, "Did you like our conversation?" She pretended not to understand and lay back on the bed seductively. He was finished with sex for the moment, but he paced the room excitedly. He took out a vial of cocaine and tapped a large amount on the mirror. She felt afraid. His eyes widened, ecstatic. He couldn't contain himself.

"You have no idea what you have just witnessed," he told her. "Someday you will remember this and tell your grandchildren you were present at this glorious moment." He started talking crazy. He couldn't stop. "Maybe we should get married and have children," he said. "It was fate that we should be together," he said, as he raised his arms to God. "Alhamdulillah! Alhamdulillah!," he shouted over and over.

She pretended to be enthralled, playing into his egomania. "You are magnificent," she told him, "like a God. What is going on, what happened on that call?"

"It was my teacher, my guide. We have done God's work. Soon the whole world will bow before us. For too long the Jews have humiliated us. They will soon know our revenge."

She continued to flatter him, hoping to learn more. "I knew when I first saw you that you were some kind of warrior."

"Yes, a holy warrior," he laughed satanically.

She wanted to leave. She felt like he was a madman. Would he let her? "Can I see you again?" she asked, as she got up off the bed and began to dress.

"Yes, yes, of course. We must." He moved towards her. She was terrified he would strangle her, but he only helped her put on her necklace. "We were meant to be together. It is Allah's will." He smiled. "Please, meet me in the bar tomorrow evening, same time, just like tonight." He kissed her, deeply, looked into her eyes. "It is meant to be."

Chapter 16

After breakfast, Frank took Ilan down to the river with his recorder running. The sky was a brilliant blue. They sat together on the sand as Frank told him about Celia's leaving and setting up her business in Abu Dhabi. But Ilan was anxious to get to the Abraham Affair.

"Frank," he said, "Celia's story is amazing. But let's skip ahead now and explain her role in the Abraham Affair. How did it start?"

Frank folded his fingers together and stretched his arms up over his head. "It began before Celia got involved, with a plan to steal an atomic bomb from the Pakistani Air Force, the 'Islamic bomb' the West and the Hindus in India had longed feared. When word of that theft landed in New Delhi, Kabul and Washington, the first question on everyone's mind was whether the safeguards put in place to prevent anyone from exploding such a device were active; most importantly, whether the trigger mechanism and the radioactive core had gone missing together. But by the end of that first day, intercepts of phone calls from Chinese technicians at the airbase in Sarghoda, where the bomb had been stored, led them to believe that the device had, indeed, been mated with its trigger. It would be difficult, but not impossible, to unlock the permissive action links, anti-tamper systems and encrypted codes designed to deactivate the bomb if not entered correctly. Done wrongly, the bomb would be disabled. Correctly, and it was ready to explode with a simple electrical switch."

Ilan looked up from his note pad and made eye contact with Frank, who then continued his story.

"The intelligence agencies concluded that the plot could only have succeeded with inside help and that, presumably, would likely include instructions for getting past the permissive action links. On the second day of the crisis, the commander of the Sarghoda air base, Brigadier General Rashid, was found dead at his desk, apparently a suicide. If he left a note, it never surfaced. He had been carefully vetted by the security division of the National Command Authority and repeatedly passed their rigorous Personnel Reliability Program. There was nothing in his record to indicate he was an Islamist, though he had been promoted after President Zia pushed the Islamization of the armed forces and there was one unconfirmed report that he had met with a senior Al Qaeda official in Peshawar."

Frank drew circles in the sand with his finger, pausing for a moment before continuing. "I doubt that was the case. I even doubt that he killed himself, but we'll never know. I met him once at a security conference when I was an analyst and found him to be highly educated, intelligent and disdainful of the 'fundis' and the jihadists, whom he referred to as 'Neanderthals.'

In any case, while the Pakistani government and military continued to deny that any of their strategic weapons were missing and adamantly refused to allow us access to verify that, other governments proceeded on the assumption that a trigger-ready tactical nuclear weapon was on the loose."

"Their greatest nightmare," Ilan noted. Frank nodded.

"The priority, obviously, was finding the bomb and determining its destination," Frank continued. "A thorough search of the area and interviews with anyone who might have witnessed the attack found nothing of value. ISI agents called in all their contacts, pressured every known jihadist leader, but weren't able to turn up a single credible lead. NSA intercepts and jihadist social media chatter were all abuzz with speculation, but they seemed as perplexed as we were. This was curious. The patterns were completely different from previous assaults on military bases. No one was taking credit for the most dramatic event since 9/11. Had I been there at the time, I would have been thinking far outside the box," Frank smiled. "But Simba and I had retired," he said petting the dog, which sat securely on his right foot.

"One of Celia's spy-escorts in Abu Dhabi overheard a phone conversation immediately after the attack between her client and someone she thought might be involved in the plot. The escort, a Brazilian beauty named Paola Vasquez, rushed to Celia's room in the Etihad Towers, the same hotel where Paola had just had the tryst with her john, a guest named Hassan Al Kidwa. She told Celia virtually word-for-word what had happened. Neither of them had heard the news about the missing Pakistani nuke, but Celia realized right away how important this might be. She called her friend at the hotel registration desk and confirmed the name Hassan Al Kidwa. Then she called her CIA contact at the US Embassy in Abu Dhabi, an old colleague of mine, and asked him to run a search on the man, supposedly a Saudi with royal family ties."

Frank laughed. "Royal family ties, my ass! Hassan Al Kidwa was a first-class shyster, a con artist, the Michael Jordan of scammers. He had no values, no ideology no fidelity to anything or anyone. Life was one transactional opportunity after another. The rap sheet on him spoke of a rough childhood. Apparently, as a child, he was forced to watch his father abuse his sister, with whom Hassan was very close."

Ilan interjected, "I would think that would be even harder to endure than being the one abused."

Frank nodded. "I agree. I heard that a few years later, the sister committed suicide. Hassan undoubtedly must have felt some guilt at not being able to protect her. He flunked out of school after that, but taught himself at least eight languages. He was actually a Jordanian, by the way, not a Saudi, as he often claimed. He turned into a great fundraiser, raised tens of millions for the mujahideen fighting the Soviets in Afghanistan, from which he skimmed a considerable percentage. He was a born seducer, loved women, revered them, and they often loved him back. He was handsome, charming, a great conversationalist and, as Paola told Celia, knew what he was doing in bed."

"How did you know him?" asked Ilan.

"The Agency worked closely with him when we were arming the mujahideen in Afghanistan. I only met him once or twice, though, when I was helping negotiate a kidnapping ransom." Frank looked at Ilan who had raised his eyebrows. "It may be U.S. government policy not to pay ransom to kidnappers," said Frank "but those rules don't apply to the CIA." Ilan nodded for him to continue.

"Paola was suspicious of Hassan. She said to Celia, 'I know a prostitute when I see one. He was good, very good, but I felt like he was acting,' she told her. 'His orgasm was real, definitely. But when he switched roles to talk on the phone, it didn't feel authentic. I'm not afraid when I'm around bad guys. I'm used to that,' she confessed. 'But I like to feel I can trust the man I'm with, good or bad. I want to know what to expect. With Hassan, he changed voices and roles like an actor.'"

Simba got up to chase a duck floating by, but the duck took off in a panic. Frank, standing, skipped some stones on the river, then sat back down and continued his story. "Although Hassan mostly raised funds for various jihadi groups, he sold information to all buyers, even the Israelis. The latest information the CIA had was that he had become a follower of a radical preacher named Zaid Hamid and was connected to Lashkar-e-Taiba, the militant network that carried out the Mumbai terrorist attacks in November 2008 that killed 160 people. One curious lead was a note from RAW, Indian intelligence, which claimed that Hassan was working for a shadowy group called Islamic Awakening Khaybar Brigades for which there was virtually no information, though one of its fliers reportedly called for Israel to be wiped off the face of the earth."

"What did Celia do with Paola's information?" asked Ilan.

Frank scratched his face and thought for a moment. "She did what I would have done," he said. "She contacted the Rat, Chaim Ratner, in Jerusalem. Ratner was probably the most deceitful person I ever met, but he had his finger in everything. He was an arbitrager of secrets. A hero in Israeli paratroop lore, he rose through the ranks to become the head of Mossad."

Ilan shook his head knowingly.

Frank went on. "Ratner was always the smartest guy in the room, ruthless when he needed to be and highly manipulative. I thought he might even be a sociopath. Undeniably brilliant, he wrote several acclaimed historical biographies including one on Moshe Dayan and another on Churchill. But he was a real Arab-hater and secretly helped start a group of young Jewish extremists who harassed and intimidated Palestinian villagers and activists, poisoned wells and desecrated mosques. He was reportedly the brains behind the so-called "Price Tag" attacks and there was some speculation that he was somehow involved in the assassination of Prime Minister Rabin. Of course, none of this was ever proven; but when an audio recording surfaced of him exhorting a group of radical settlers not to stop until they expelled every last Palestinians from Judea and Samaria, he was summarily dismissed and disgraced."

He paused for a moment and smiled, raising his eyebrows. "It was the best thing that ever happened to him, though. He parlayed his unequaled access to intelligence operatives around the world into a market for the sale and purchase of secrets. He became fabulously wealthy."

Ilan hurriedly scribbled notes on a pad, even though he was recording the conversation. Frank continued without pause. "When he caught word of Celia's prostitute ring, he was immediately intrigued. A private intelligence-gathering agency was right in his ballpark. Besides, he loved prostitutes, was obsessed by them. He had been a protégé of the great, late diplomat Abba Eban, who reportedly owned the largest library of pornographic films in the world. They would frequently drink Scotch, smoke cigars and watch porn together in Eban's upstairs viewing room. Ratner was careful to stay away from hookers while in the Mossad, but as a private citizen, he indulged frequently until prostate surgery left him impotent. He invited Celia to meet with him in Jerusalem and, although disappointed that she was not herself a prostitute, was hugely impressed with her. He became a regular client and even fancied himself a mentor."

"Sounds like a fascinating character," interjected Ilan. "I remember reading about him when he got drummed out of Mossad, but I never heard any description of the man. He seemed to have disappeared after the scandal." He motioned for Frank to continue.

"When she called Ratner to tell him she had important information to share, she was unaware of the news that was just breaking. Ratner understood how her story connected to the attack at Sargodha. He knew he could buy her information at a huge discount from what it would be worth once she found out its real value, but he read to her what was scrolling on the bottom of his television screen at that very moment, and offered to help guide her next steps. He promised her a $50,000 down payment against future commissions. He did not ask for exclusivity, which surprised Celia, but suggested they go in as partners."

"She asked him what they should do next. Ratner told her to have Paola try to meet with Hassan again and learn what she could. He would arrange very discreet surveillance. Celia began to insist that it was too dangerous to involve Paola anymore, but Paola begged her to let her continue the operation. Reluctantly, Celia gave in; but she told Ratner there must be no eavesdropping, nothing that could alert Hassan that he was being watched."

Chapter 17

Paola arrived the next evening at the Tower's bar and took up her perch on the corner stool. Dressed in a sleeveless, tight fitting white silk sheath, cut low in back, her most seductive outfit, she looked stunning with a pair of dangling zirconium earrings. There was no sign of Hassan. She almost decided not to wear this outfit, expecting it unlikely he would seek her out again. Discreetly, she searched the room to see if she were being watched. The bar was mostly empty. She was nervous, glancing frequently at her watch. She didn't touch the shrimp cocktail in front of her.

A man in a dark blue suit approached. "Are you Ms. Vasquez, by any chance?"

Her heart beat faster. She nodded. He handed her a phone. She held it to her ear while she looked around the room, not sure what to expect. It was Hassan.

"Hello, my dear. Please excuse me, but I would rather not be seen in public tonight. Would you be free to come to my room? I would love to talk with you."

David Hoffman

The man in the suit was staring at her. All men did. He turned when she noticed him. She looked around the room again to see who else might be watching. "How did you know my last name?" she asked in a low voice.

"It's my job to know everything," he joked.

She was not amused. She sensed something wrong. "I'll call my service to let them know I'm with you," she said, hung up abruptly and handed the phone back. She considered bailing, but took the elevator to the 56th floor.

He was waiting outside the door to his room. She glanced inside and called Celia, put the phone back in her white patent leather purse on mute, but didn't hang up.

"What is your job that you would find out my name?" she demanded. She would let him know she was upset. The first rule of survival for sex workers is to remain in charge.

He looked at her sympathetically. She was spectacular, even sexier when she was mad. He knew all about her, knew she shared secrets with Celia, figured she knew all about him by now, as well. "My business is helping people. Not very different from yours, I suppose. I connect people who have a great deal of money with those who are fighting for their dignity in my adopted country, Pakistan, for all Muslims who have been humiliated." It would be best to be honest with her more or less, he calculated; since she would know about him anyway, better to gain her trust. "Please, do not be alarmed," he said. "I did not mean to stalk you. It is only," he searched for the right phrase, "I must be careful with whom I meet. You must understand."

She looked at him sternly and then smiled coquettishly. She took a step towards him, closed the door with her foot behind her, dropped her handbag on the floor and kissed him. His breath was sweet. She opened her eyes. His were closed; then they opened, meeting hers. They stared deeply, measuring each other. She tried to discern how much of him was real, how much an act. He knew hers was all an act, but he wanted it anyway. She felt him getting hard, pressed up against him for a moment and then stepped back. "You look terrible," she said. "What's wrong?"

He glanced at himself in the mirror. "I've been up all night," he said. "My work can be pretty stressful at times. Besides, I drank too much and too much blow. How are you?"

She smiled, pirouetted. She was dazzling. "I'm great."

He stepped towards her, took her in his arms and kissed her tenderly on her lips, her forehead, her eyes and then her mouth again. He was a connoisseur. She could tell he knew more about her than her name. This was a game, maybe a deadly one, but she rose to the challenge.

"So, you are a terrorist?" she asked, provoking him. "Or just their financial advisor?"

He was taken aback. *I like this woman*, he thought. He smiled impishly. "Some people say 'terrorist;' for others we are 'freedom fighters.' The Americans dropped an atomic bomb, two of them actually. They killed two hundred thousand people. Do we call them 'terrorists' for that? No, they are the victors." He paused for a moment, judging her reaction. "You know, some would call you a 'whore,' but I prefer the word 'escort.' Personally, I think women like you should be revered. You should be put on a pedestal."

She removed her earrings and placed them on the bedside table. Two could play this game. "Did you know that in biblical times, in Jerusalem, there were 'Holy Prostitutes' who were hired by the temple?" she said.

He smiled. "How do you know so much about Jews?" he asked, cocking his head at her.

"I like Jews. They are great lovers," she answered and sat on the bed.

He laughed, "That's because they are really just Arabs. Oh, they speak a different language; but they are one of us, just another Arab tribe. Right now, they are on top. Once we were and we massacred them. Mohammed slaughtered them at the Battle of Khaybar. Our time will come again."

Enough talking about politics. Time to change the subject to sex, she thought. She had provoked him enough. She patted the bed, gesturing for him to sit beside her. "Arabs can be great lovers, too," she added. "But you are unusual. I feel you respect us. Many Arabs I've known don't. They are so hypocritical. They talk about women as if we are holy objects that must be protected, covered up; but then they pay a neighborhood Imam to give them a 'temporary marriage' license for an hour. All you do is say a prayer, and you are free to buy sex."

He sat next to her. "That's the Shiites," he said. "They are all whores."

"And you? You Sunnis? You keep your four wives. Who's a whore?"

He laughed again, put his arms around her. "You are a tiger. You will make me fall in love with you. I was drunk when I suggested we get married last night. Now I am sober. Maybe we should."

He kissed her passionately. They fell back on the bed together. He asked if she wanted cocaine. She shook her head. They kissed some more. Then she stood up and turned her back for him to unzip her.

The sex was good, very good. He took his time with her. She pretended to have multiple orgasms. It excited him. Finally, he came with a piercing cry. He lay on his back breathing hard. "Alhamdulilla!" he repeated over and over.

They showered together. He massaged every inch of her. She got turned on despite herself. But he took it no further and they moved from the bathroom into the bedroom toweling off. He flipped on the television. The story was about the attack at Sarghoda and the missing nuke. "Investigators now think it had to be an inside job," said the reporter on CNN. "Brigadier General Akram Rashid, the commander of the Sarghoda air base, was found dead at his desk, apparently a suicide. No note has been found."

Hassan buried his face in his hands. When he lifted his eyes again, his flesh had turned ashen. His eyes teared. He repeated some prayer she couldn't understand. She put her arms around him.

"Hassan, what's wrong?" she said.

"I knew him. He was my friend, almost a father to me. I helped his wife get surgery she needed. She is just recovering now. Oh my God!" He cried real tears. She held him. This was no act.

Chapter 18

Adorned with medals and ribbons, fifteen generals from India's military and intelligence services sat glumly around a large oval table in an underground bunker reserved for war. General Dalbir Sing, Chief of COAS, the Army Staff, reminded the group that this was not an exercise.

The suicide of Brigadier General Akram Rashid worried him. Rashid was a professional soldier, not some crazy jihadist. If he were responsible in any way for this operation, its ultimate target would be India, not Afghanistan, as some had speculated. Having a nuclear weapon hidden somewhere in New Delhi would give Pakistan an advantage that could be used to trump whatever anti-missile defenses India might mount in the future. In a single stroke it would nullify any potential for an Indian first strike that might preemptively neutralize Pakistan's large arsenal of nuclear weapons. *Brilliant!* he thought.

'Brilliant, but why would he kill himself?' General Sing wondered. 'Or was he perhaps killed?' It was unlike Rashid to attack his own soldiers. Above everything else he was loyal to the troops in his command. On a strategic level Sing could understand the move. But on a human level, it made no sense.

He looked around the table. The usual arrogance of his generals was gone. They looked scared. Their expensive hardware systems would be of little use in this situation. He stared at Rajinder Khanna, the chief of RAW, the Research and Analysis Wing, India's intelligence agency, but Khanna would not make eye contact with him. Khanna was clearly embarrassed. How had he not anticipated this attack? How could he turn up no leads? They had spent hundreds of billions of rupees infiltrating every jihadist network, every layer of the Pakistani government and military, and now they had nothing to show for it. *I should take his head,* General Sing thought. *But it's me they'll blame.* He had no good options.

He wondered how many of these officers even comprehended what a 50-kiloton tactical nuclear weapon could do to New Delhi and its 16 million people. He pressed the clicker in his hand and the first slide came to life on a large screen at the end of the table. It showed a map of New Delhi with four concentric rings around ground zero at India Gate. Everything from that point out, covering the entire area inside India Gate Circle, would be vaporized in a giant fireball. Huge amounts of radioactive fallout would spew from the surface.

From the Indira Gandhi National Center for the Arts in the West to Major Dhayan Chand National Stadium to the East, virtually every living thing would die from the force of the blast. Out 1.64 kilometers past the National Science Centre to the intersection of Red Cross Road and Rafi Ahmed

Kidwai Marj, all residential buildings would collapse. People would be exposed to a 500-rem radiation dose with mortality rates of 50 to 90%. Dying would take between several hours and several weeks. East over the Yarmuna River West to the Presidential Estate, a radius of 2.87 kilometers, citizens would suffer third degree burns. Overall, estimated fatalities were 249,940, including most of the men seated around that table. A chastened silence filled the room.

The head of the Research and Analysis Wing spoke up, "This is clearly a military operation. If it were the fundis, we'd know about it. We should respond in kind."

"And how do you propose to do that?" General Sing asked.

"We could sneak our own nuke into Islamabad and let them know we would not hesitate to act," he answered.

Most of the generals shook their heads in disapproval. It was madness. Besides, they still had the full capacity to respond to any attack with their superior arsenal and missiles.

"This is exactly like the Cuban Missile Crisis," one of the older generals commented. "Kennedy convinced the Soviets to remove their nuclear missiles not by threat, but by offering to remove American rockets from Turkey."

No one liked this idea. "Kennedy went to the United Nations," said another. "Maybe we should do the same."

A bald naval officer whose head seemed to rest on his shoulders without benefit of a neck seethed with anger. "This is crazy. Maybe we should offer to massage their feet. Appeasement will just feed their hunger. This is a blatant provocation. It is a time for us to be strong. Kennedy blockaded Cuba. Perhaps we should blockade Karachi." The room was silent. A scent of danger was in the air.

While this debate went on, ending without a conclusion, a similar meeting was taking place in Rawalpindi. The Pakistani generals were apoplectic. How could they lose control over one of their nukes? This was their number one security issue, their absolute highest priority. Already humiliated by the Americans when they snatched Osama Bin Laden from under their noses, they were in utter despair. All of them offered their resignations. They had let down the nation. Fifteen of their commandos killed. All of the enemy escaping without harm. Time and time again they had tried to reassure the other nuclear powers that they could protect their arsenal, their crown jewels, that there was no possibility of them falling into the hands of terrorists. Now they had failed. Or had they?

General Raheel Sharif, the Chief of Staff of the Army, was perplexed. He had ordered a top-secret inventory of their nuclear weapons and found nothing missing. It didn't make sense. The exact number and location of these weapons were Pakistan's greatest secret. The commanders of each of the sixteen bases where they were kept had real-time knowledge of their own inventories, but a detailed master list was not kept for fear it might someday leak out. It was better to keep their enemies guessing. All these commanders were brought in to Rawalpindi to report directly to their commanding general. All swore they had 100% control over these bombs. Of course, General Rashid was dead. The missing weapon came from his base at Sarghoda. But his deputy swore on his life that all were accounted for. Sometimes dummy bombs were moved to fool any surveillance, but only General Rashid would have known about this. They did not keep records of such things.

There was no assuaging the Americans, the Indians or anyone else. The military, the government and the intelligence agencies could swear on their mothers' graves to no avail. Even if they allowed others to make their own accounting—which of course they could not—they would still assume they were being lied to. Pakistan's humiliation was total. General Sharif ordered his ISI chief to cooperate to the fullest extent possible with the intelligence branches of allies and adversaries alike. The only way to rectify this tragedy was to find the bomb and disable it. Every effort must be made to identify the perpetrators of this plot. It almost had to be foreign agents. But how was General Rashid involved? His wife, he had just learned, was in an Israeli hospital. Could that just be a coincidence or were the Jews behind this?

Chapter 19

Celia and Paola arrived together at the law office of Kroger, Kroger and Jamison, which represented Celia, as well as her girls from time to time. The firm kept a secure conference room for its clients, several of whom had important confidential information they needed to discuss in secret. The view from the office was so high it made Celia nervous. Abu Dhabi was like that, the powerful competing to see who could rise above the others. *To be closer to God?* wondered Celia, *or* as far away from Hell as they could get?

Chaim Ratner texted to say he was delayed in heavy traffic, but would arrive in five minutes. Coffee and bottled water arrived. A moment later Ratner walked in. A bookish looking man in his seventies, of medium height, with short curly dark hair, obviously dyed, and wearing tortoise shell glasses, Ratner exuded the self-confidence one would expect of a former Director of the Mossad. He greeted Celia warmly with a kiss on both cheeks. His face lit up when he saw Paola, who rose from her chair and extended her hand to shake his. He held it a moment too long. She had a visceral dislike of this person, but gave her best-practiced smile.

He looked around the room approvingly. "Good choice," he said. Paola had a fine-tuned sensitivity to men, which bordered on the paranormal. She felt immediately that this toad-looking man was not to be trusted. She had learned not to go into a room alone with such a man as this, but here she was knee deep in a political intrigue with him she hardly understood. She looked at Celia with some alarm, but Celia did not show the same concern.

"Let's get down to business," said Ratner. "Timing is all-important in the arbitrage business. We have something valuable to sell, but its due date could expire at any moment and become worthless." He turned to look at Celia seated on his right. "Right now, we may be the only ones who have any leads at all about the group behind this operation. No one has taken credit for it yet, but they will eventually. Even Al Qaeda stayed quiet right after 9/11. But I suspect whatever terrorist organization pulled this off, if there were one, will soon do something to prove they have possession of the bomb. That is, if they intend to use it as a bargaining chip. If they only want to punish someone, they may not." He looked at them both, puffed up with his own brilliance. He reminded Celia of Henry Kissinger.

"If there were one?" asked Paola, repeating what he had just said.

He would give anything to have sex with this woman, he thought, would have paid any price. But those days are gone, regrettably. He shrugged, gesturing with his hands open, eyes lifted. "Well, it could be a military operation. It was highly professional. Maybe India, maybe the Pakistanis themselves, for whatever meshugga reasons. Personally, I doubt it. If it were ever discovered, their governments would pay dearly. It's too big a risk."

He stopped to drink some water he poured in a glass before continuing. "But I admit to being surprised by this whole caper. I telephoned my best contacts in Islamabad. No one seemed to know anything. That's highly unusual for Pakistan. Sometimes I think their whole economy runs on what we pay informants there." He smiled at himself. "Everything about this feels like an inside job. If it were one of the usual suspects, the chatter would be deafening. Instead, there's silence."

Turning to Celia, he asked "So, what do we know?"

Celia swiveled in her seat to face him squarely. "According to my contact at the U.S. Embassy, Hassan Al Kidwa's last known affiliation was with a jihadist group called Islamic Awakening Khaybar Brigades." Ratner's eyebrows arched. "Little, if anything, is known of them," she said.

Paola broke in, "He mentioned to me something about the Battle of Khaybar. Could that have any connection?"

Ratner frowned, tapped his finger on his lips. "The battle of Khaybar was one of Mohammed's first victories," he explained. "Khaybar was the largest Jewish settlement at the time, heavily fortified. Ali, the man the Shiites revere as the successor to Mohammed, was the hero of that battle, but Sunnis celebrate it as well. They're proud to have defeated the

Jews there. But its main significance was Mohammed's demand that the Jews evacuate the area."

"Do you know anything about this group?" Paola asked.

"No, I've never heard of them," Ratner replied, "but that doesn't mean anything. The jihadis make up all sorts of names to hide who they are or pretend they are many when they are few. The same group may reinvent itself dozens of times. For the time being, this may be all we've got, but it's worth a great deal of money. What else do we know?"

"Not much," Paola answered "except perhaps a feeling I had about Hassan. There was something about his manner that seemed like an act to me. I'm not sure why. It could've been all the cocaine he had snorted. It felt like he was trying to impress the person on the other line, or me." She shrugged her shoulders. "Last night, just before I left, we watched the news about that general committing suicide."

"Yes, Akram Rashid," Ratner added.

"Well," continued Paola, "Hassan broke down when he heard this news. I don't know if that's important. But I could tell it really shook him. He wasn't acting."

Ratner bit one of his nails. He didn't mention he knew General Rashid or that he had called him shortly after the news first broke about the missing bomb.

"I know Hassan Al Kidwa," said Ratner, "dealt with him several times. He's no ideologue. He'll do anything for money."

"What do we do now?" asked Celia.

Ratner played with the pencil on his pad, rubbing the sharp point against his thumb, deep in thought. "The simplest thing would be to hold an auction, sell this to the highest bidder. Or," he paused for a moment, considering the options, "or we could run this operation ourselves. We could sell what we know now, but not reveal our source. If we work Hassan," he looked intensely at Paola, "we keep control of our asset. If the big intelligence agencies get involved, they'll turn it into a circus. Information will leak out. He'll know he's being followed. Right now, we can keep this discreet, between us. He obviously likes Paola." *Who wouldn't?* he thought.

"That's fine," said Celia, "but no wires. I don't care if it's a nuclear bomb, I won't put her at risk."

"OK, understood. But we've got to tap his phone, find out who he's communicating with in Pakistan. That'll be crucial. I know some experts in Beirut who could come here immediately. They're the best. He'll never know he was being surveilled. There would be no connection to Paola or to you. But we'll need to act quickly."

Celia drummed her fingers on the table. *I don't like this,* she thought. *We should just sell what we know and get out of this mess.* "How do we convince anyone that the scoop we've got now is a legitimate lead, if we won't explain how we came across it?" she asked. "We can't just tell the CIA or the Indians we overheard a conversation, but we can't tell you who it was with."

Ratner smiled. "You're right," he said. "Without some proof, we could just be pissing in the wind. It's all about trust. Frankly, the Americans don't trust me at all. But my own government does, whatever else they might say in public. General Lonzman's head of the Military Intelligence Directorate.

I got him his job. He'll not only believe me, he'll do whatever I ask of him. He'll let me run this thing my way. The Americans ultimately are most important. You'll need to do that sell, Celia. I think they'll believe you. They already know you asked about Hassan, so they'll be onto him. You'll need to get them to promise to keep their distance, though. In the meantime, let me see what kind of deal I might get from Mordechai Lonzman. He may resell it to the Indians or ISI, or probably trade them for something. It'll be worth plenty to them. Costs will not be a consideration."

Celia's fear rose in her chest. She had never gotten so directly involved before. All she had done was sell information she picked up from her girls. Now, she was in over her head and she knew it. Most of all, she worried about Paola. It was her life that was on the line. *I need Frank,* she thought.

Chapter 20

We were alone and silent on the long elevator ride down from our meeting at the lawyer's office. Both of us looked shell shocked. My heart was racing out of control. My stomach felt like it was seasick. I could see the tightness in Paola's jaw. We did not make eye contact. A pair of smartly dressed men opened the large glass doors in the foyer for us. The heat of the day assaulted us. Reaching the pavement, we turned to face each other, eyes the mirror of fear. Then, spontaneously, we broke into laughter, laughter that shook the core of us till tears washed down our cheeks.

It took a couple minutes to catch our breath and regain our composure. We looked at each other and started up again. "How the fuck did we get ourselves in this mess?" Paola asked.

I shook my head. "I'm sorry, Paola."

"I mean, I'm a whore from the favelas. I wasn't exactly trained to stop a group of terrorists with a nuclear bomb," she continued. "I used to think I'd become a dentist. This is insane."

"And now you're a spy selling secrets to Israeli intelligence and the CIA. I never realized whores had balls."

"We're both crazy, you know," said Paola. "If we were rational, we'd walk away from this, let this ugly guy Ratner take it from here. I don't like that man. He's slimy. He makes my skin crawl."

"I don't trust him, either, but he's always been reliable. And he pays well." As I said this, though, I realized that the money didn't really matter to me. Yes, I was a businesswoman, proud of it. I loved being an entrepreneur, but it was success more than money that really motivated me. "Is it worth it though?" I asked.

"Celia, I'm a prostitute. I rent out my body to men for money. There's always some risk, but nothing like this. I don't feel like we have any control. We're out of our league." She looked up at the sky, nervously. Then she turned to Celia and smiled. "But, you know what? I love how insanely audacious we are, a couple of smart-ass women taking on the whole male world, with their nukes and their power and their penises."

"I know what you mean," I laughed. "It's the audacity that's got me, too. We're good, girl. You and me. We make a great team. I feel like we're starring in some action film. I expect Matt Damon to come along any second on a motorcycle. But one false move on our part and we'll end up as pet food. We need someone who knows this shit." I paused for a moment. "I think I know just the man, Frank Reynolds."

"Is he that dude you left in California? The one whose wife was blown up?" she asked.

"Yeah, Frank's the best there is. I don't know if I can reach him. But if he'd help us, I'd feel a lot better about our safety."

I tried to imagine Frank's reaction, pictured him there with Simba working on his model boat, raking the apples in the orchard. 'Did he still have the phone I gave him? Would it be charged? Would he come even if I reached him?' "I'll try and call him."

"What do you think Hassan's up to?" Paola asked. "What's his target? Blow up New York?"

"I guess that's what we need to find out," I answered. "Part of me says to do this for the money. This is a business deal, nothing more. But part of me still wants to save the world from itself. I'm a hopeless romantic."

Paola smiled, "You can take the girl out of Cuba, but ..."

She was right. I had to be careful. I knew that. You can try to change the world and you end up getting fucked. The game's too dangerous for any innocence. Too many lives at stake, including Paola's and mine. *We're good, but we've got to be perfect,* I thought. "I think we'll do best if we treat this as a business opportunity. Leave the politics to others. Frank once told me he approached intelligence like science or journalism. Our job is to get the facts, if we can, not get involved with our emotions, separate ourselves from the drama."

"Are you sure you were never a prostitute?" Paola kidded. "That's what we do all the time."

We hailed a cab and each went our separate ways home from there. Paola had left it with Hassan to call her. She had given him her cell phone number. There'd be little we could do, if he didn't call. But something told me he would. She was exquisitely sensitive to men's feelings and she felt confident that Hassan needed her.

I went back to the Towers feeling drained. I was making decisions that put Paola's life in danger. If anything happened to her, I didn't know how I'd live with myself. I guess that's what Frank experienced with his wife. I loved Paola as a sister, as a best friend. I couldn't let anything happen to her.

When I got to my apartment, I turned on the bath and called my contact at the U.S. Embassy. Our phones were encrypted, but I simply told him I had something he'd want, something for sale. We arranged for him to come right over. I looked at the clock. It would be midnight in California. Frank would be asleep, hopefully in his cabin, not in the outdoor bed where he wouldn't hear the phone, if, indeed it was charged. I hesitated. *Maybe I should meet with the American first, make sure this game was really in play,* I thought.

I took a bath and waited by the front doors in the air conditioning for him to pick me up, as we had arranged. A black sedan with tinted windows pulled up and I got inside. We spoke only in pleasantries as we drove to a nearby park. I made him promise before telling him anything that from this point on everything would have to follow my rules. I explained that I had information about the missing bomb in Pakistan. It would cost him $50,000. If he didn't think it was worth it, he could have it for free; but there'd be no more. If he liked what he got, I would have more to sell. But only if he did nothing to compromise our source, no surveillance, no eavesdropping.

"Is it Hassan Al Kidwa?" he asked. I knew he'd suspect that since I had asked about him just two days ago. I shrugged.

"Do we have a deal?" I asked.

"You're really sure you've got something?"

"I am. I'll let you be the judge of that," I answered.

He nodded his head. "Mind if I record this?" he asked, taking out a small tape recorder.

"I assumed you were," I said. We shook hands. Americans feel comfortable when they can shake hands. I told him about the phone call on the first night, but never used Paola's name. I didn't tell him about Hassan's reaction to the news about General Rashid's suicide on the subsequent night. I saved that for later, in case we needed more bait. His eyes told me this was big, very big, probably worth far more than we were asking. He understood we had an exclusive lead. We had a line on the Who, but there was the What, the Where and the When still to discover.

"Celia, I think you know how important this could be." His voice quivered slightly. "We simply have to surveil his phone. We've got to know who he's talking to."

I assured him we already had that covered. He'd get that as soon as we knew something, "in the next installment," I said. He looked at me skeptically. We had done business before, but nothing on this scale. He had no reason to think I could handle something like this. I figured he was already thinking how to run the surveillance without my knowledge. There was simply no way the CIA could let an amateur like me run an operation on something that might be many times bigger than 9/11.

"I can't do this, Celia," he admitted. "I could promise you anything, but Langley would never agree to it, not in a million years. I'll get you the $50,000, but we have no choice but to monitor this guy. We've always trusted each other and I don't want to lie to you now."

"I appreciate that," I said. "Give me six hours. I have a team arriving any minute from Beirut, Mossad's best wiremen, who will tap his phones. I will give you direct access to them, but it will cost you."

"Money's no object. Just name your price. I'll give you two hours. It may take that long for my bosses to decide what they want to do. I'll hold them off for as long as I can after that," he said. I could tell he was impressed that I had some subcontractors coming from Mossad.

"I'm bringing Frank Reynolds into this," I bluffed.

His mouth dropped open. "Frank Reynolds? Are you serious?" I smiled coyly. We left it at that. It was blazingly hot outside in the park, but that didn't account for all his perspiring. This would be the biggest scoop of his career.

When I got back to my room, I poured myself a strong drink, something I never did. I was shaking inside. When I calmed down, I picked up the phone and dialed the number I had long ago memorized. It rang eight times. *At least he has it charged,* I thought. But just before I put the receiver down, I heard his voice, sleepy but clear, "Celia?"

Chapter 21

The CIA and Mossad had a 24-hour head start on the name of the alleged hijackers, the so-called Khaybar Brigades, but little to show for it. Israel traded the tip to Pakistan in return for a list of two-dozen Palestinians who had trained with the Haqqani network. Pakistani informants sold the information to the Indians for a pittance and who then sold what little they knew to the Chinese and the Russians. Celia, Paola and Chaim Ratner split $100,000. Only the CIA, though, knew of Celia's involvement, with Ratner as the gatekeeper. But the Khaybar Brigades, if they existed at all, left no traces of their origins or their ultimate purpose.

Alive with the laughter of raucous young boys, the yellow school bus rumbled along the clay road off the Sarghoda-Faisalabad highway. It stopped, as it always did, by an abandoned grain elevator where a knot of kids waited in their blue uniforms, then turned toward the old farmhouse up the road. A tall man emerged carrying an insulated cold box and passed out ice cream sandwiches to the squealing youngsters while other men loaded a steel container into a special compartment in the back of the bus that had been outfitted in the space where the last two rows of seats had been.

The bus returned to the highway and approached the checkpoint at its usual time at 8:05am. The guards made a cursory search with long-handled mirrors under the chassis and waved the driver through. The boys poured out of the bus when it arrived at the school in Faisalabad and the driver continued on his long journey to the port city of Muhammad Bin Qasim, trailed by two car loads of armed men. Once out of Faisalabad the driver called a prearranged number to alert them that all was well. It was time to release the video that would make the world tremble.

The video was as slick as the fighting had been professional. The sounds of "Allahu Akhbar" and the roar of motorcycles mixed with the deafening staccato of AK47s, a ball of fire engulfed the green lorry as it crashed and exploded into the white SUV. There was a close-up of a fighter, face wrapped in a checkered scarf, firing a rocket propelled grenade, a swarm of Fedayeen on motorbikes picking off hapless commandos in slow motion, a choreography of blood. And then, silence for three long seconds before a disembodied voice in English counted down, 'ten, nine, eight'... while four bearded men, like pallbearers, slid a gleaming oval-shaped stainless-steel container from a white van, 'three, two, one'...and then a sound from hell as a mushroom cloud spread its terrifying beauty, the bomb rising ever higher into the sky as a script in Arabic and English scrolled below. "Martyrdom is for the glory of Allah, Islamic Awakening Khaybar Brigades."

Within seconds the two-minute video spread virally, like the fission of atoms in the bomb it depicted, from a jihadi website to every corner of the earth. It coursed through social media and was broadcast in the perpetual loops of 24-hour television news to hundreds of millions of people. Although the story of the theft of the bomb had been big news when it first happened, it slowly faded from the front pages, as there were no new developments, no video to document the event and adamant denials from the Pakistani military that anything was amiss. There could be no denial now. The only real question for most people was where the bomb was headed. "We are all hostage" screamed a headline in the Guardian.

Fear is contagious. In editorials, on social media and in mainstream news something fundamental shifted, a recognition that some terrible threshold had been crossed and the world had entered an even darker and more dangerous time than it had on 9/11. Extremists called for pre-emptive nuclear strikes on Pakistan, though there was no evidence that the bomb was still there. Others threatened retaliation should the bomb be used. A Twitter hashtag #bombthehaj gathered millions of followers who searched for a way to restore the Cold War balance of deterrence, seen now as halcyon days. On television there were endless graphics depicting the potential destruction of a fifty-kiloton bomb on various cities around the world and broadcasts of Peter Watkins' 1965 film classic, *The War Game*, which originally was banned for its graphic representation of the effects of a nuclear bomb. At ports and transport terminals, already heightened security measures were doubled and tripled.

But a sense of inevitability hung over the world like a gathering storm.

Chapter 22

At home in her apartment, sparsely furnished in modern comforts of leather and steel, Paola silently wept as she watched the evening news. She was completely overcome. The entire world was preoccupied with events of apocalyptic dimensions and she, little Paola Vasquez, who never graduated from high school, was at the very center of things. She shook from the immensity of what she had become a part of. There was no one to comfort her. There could be no one. She was all alone.

She wanted to run away. The burden was too great. Somehow, she felt guilty for stepping into this. Had she been anything other than a prostitute, she would have had no involvement with this madness. The bravado she experienced leaving the lawyers office was gone. She was the bait in a deadly game. Absolutely nothing in her background could prepare her for this role. She and Celia were insane to take this on, she knew. They should have passed on the information and called it quits. The cashier's check for $25,000 on her dresser confirmed her mistake.

She reached for the phone and started to dial Celia to call it off, but hung up. God how she wanted a cigarette, a habit she had quit six months before. She tried looking at herself in the mirror, but couldn't. She knew she had low self-esteem. Sure, she could cite all the passages about the Holy Prostitutes of biblical times, but *a whore is just a whore*, Hassan had reminded her. She had done all right for herself, though. She had beautiful clothes, a fine apartment, travelled whenever she felt like it. She worked when she wanted, turned down customers she didn't like and was damn good at what she did. Her girlfriends had mostly gotten married and had kids and she had no one she could confide in. She knew she should get out more, date some nice men; but that whole game reminded her too much of work. It was confusing to know how to conduct herself on a real date. Her life was an act and a secret. She was losing touch with her true self.

And now this. She knew nothing about politics, rarely listened to the news. What good could she do? But despite her fears and loathing, way down deep inside her a small tender voice told her she could do it, that this was her moment to be something she could be proud of. She had handled things well so far, hadn't she? Hassan might have tripped someone else up. If it weren't for her, there would be no clue to the perpetrators of this crime. She thought she had touched some place real in Hassan through all his bullshit. She was confident he would call her again. She was no less an actor than he. They were equals in this play. If there were information to be had from him, she would get it. She might be a whore, but she was a damn good one, the best. But what if she failed?

When she was a little girl sleeping next to her mother on a cardboard mattress in the favela in Brazil, she dreamed she would be Joan of Arc, pure and strong, clad in gold, bathed in the light of the sun. When her mother wasn't drunk she told little Paola stories of princesses with magic powers, beautiful princesses dressed in silks for whom princes and heroes risked their lives to marry. She used to think she had a destiny to do something great. That little girl still lived somewhere inside her, but the princes had become rich men who paid for her favors with money, not with their lives. She felt ashamed, even as she felt proud to have escaped the favela and prospered. Perhaps this business with Hassan and the bomb was her opportunity for redemption, a way to wash away her sins.

She had no belief in religion, though she wished she had. She wanted to pray, but had no idea how. It was all so much bigger than she was. She envied Celia who seemed so sure of herself, so much in control. Paola had only herself to believe in. She felt she must walk through a wall of fire. The little girl's voice inside her told her not to be afraid. For the first time in her life she thought she might believe in God. She was riding a wave much bigger than herself. She would surrender to her fate. She would walk through the fire. Crawling into a fetal position on the floor, she prayed for help.

Chapter 23

"Yes. Oh God, thank you for answering," Celia said, her breath heavy.

"Are you alright?" Frank asked.

"I am, but I need your help."

"What's wrong?" Frank sat up and lit the kerosene lamp next to his bed. He remembered her saying, 'I'll only call if it were an issue of life and death.' He could hear the weight of her breath across an ocean of time and space.

She began crying, like a soft rain, fearful but relieved. "I need you." She had told herself not to sound so desperate, so needy, but she was. "I'm in something way over my head." She paused a moment to catch her breath. "I don't want to talk about it on the phone. But maybe you've heard about it, the news from Pakistan." When he didn't answer, she laughed. "You're probably the only person on earth who hasn't."

"How can I help?" he asked.

She hadn't thought exactly what she would say. She hadn't really expected him to answer, figured his phone would not be charged. "Frank, can you catch the next plane to Abu Dhabi? I can have a ticket waiting for you. I really can't explain anything on the phone. You'll just have to trust me." He didn't answer. "Do you still have a valid passport?" she asked.

"Celia," he said. "I've missed you a lot."

She let out a long breath. "I've missed you, too, Frank." Her heart was racing. She held a hand over her mouth, stifling a cry. "Please come here," she pleaded in a little girl's voice. "I need you."

The regional airport was an hour and a half away. She called back five minutes later. He would just have time to catch the first flight to San Francisco and then board an Emirates flight to Abu Dhabi.

He hung up and stared at himself in the little square mirror above his dresser. The man staring back at him looked ancient. The face seemed to talk back to him. *Time to saddle up*, it said. He examined his eyes. In the yellow light of the kerosene lamp they looked grey. He breathed deeply, expanding his chest. Then he grabbed a pair of scissors hanging above him and chopped away at the savage white beard that had been his companion since he escaped from civilization years ago. He watched the transformation like a bystander at a sporting event as he shaved his face clean. His expression came alive. He couldn't help but smile at himself. He reached up and cut his hair off above his ears. Twenty years seemed to drop from him in a pile on the floor of his tiny hut. He took a roll of twenties from a coffee can on a high shelf he kept for emergencies, grabbed his passport, threw a change of underwear and a sweater into a gym bag and strode over to the truck. Four hours later he was in a first-class seat flying over the ocean.

Celia waited anxiously at the arrivals door, scanning the crowd as they disembarked. She worried what he would look like in this environment. She feared she might have made a mistake. "Celia," she heard a familiar voice next to her. She hardly recognized him. He looked just like the man she had met in her hotel room in Mexico years before. The same sharp blue eyes, the steady kind face, the easy alertness. She wanted to leap into his arms, to melt into him, but, restraining herself, turned her cheek for a polite kiss.

"Do you have any bags?" she asked.

"Are you kidding?" he smiled.

They walked without speaking past the glittering counters of jewelry for sale, past all the brand name clothing shops. He had never seen such an obscene display of wealth. He could not be further from his home than this, he thought.

On the plane ride over he had worried that he might not recognize her. It bothered him that he could not conjure up her face more easily. His lack of visual memory was an impairment, he knew. When he thought of her, which he did often every day, he pictured a photograph of her. Would she be as beautiful as he remembered her in the one photo he had of her at the beach?

When finally he did spot her, standing alone outside of customs with all the people waiting for their loved ones and the chauffeurs holding signs, she did not seem to recognize him. When he came near her, even the scent of her was familiar.

At the exit, glass doors opened into the late afternoon furnace of a desert sandstorm.

"Welcome to Abu Dhabi," she said.

They got in a cab and rode through the swirling sand past a landscape that seemed surreal to him. Skyscrapers, largely empty he noticed, poked rudely into the grey sky. Men in white bishts and kaffiyehs mixed with men in tailored suits. Women were veiled and not. There were miniskirts alongside abeyas and naqibs. Of laborers and the poor, he saw none. The police seemed everywhere. This was an oasis of wealth and order, he knew; but the extent of it surprised him. It seemed a parody of itself.

"What did you do with Simba?" she asked.

He pretended to be shocked. "Simba? Shit, I forgot." He waited a moment for the joke to take effect. "No, I left him with Tom. He'll be fine there."

They talked about the normal things people discuss when they haven't seen each other for so long, nothing about the issue at hand. He could sense her loneliness. She seemed different than before, perhaps more confident, more self-sufficient. She was amazed at how easily he adapted to his environment and found herself surprised at the physical attraction she felt for him. His body was lean and athletic. His hands were rough. The sharpness of his crystal blue eyes had not faded. There was something canine about him. She would have fun helping him pick out clothes. The taxi left them off in front of her hotel.

"I'm sure you'll want a shower," she said.

"That can wait," he responded. "Let's go for a walk. I want to hear what's going on and I never trust hotels. The walls are all wired. I should know."

Celia's face brightened. This was the Frank she had wanted here. "Let me call Paola. She's been waiting in my room to meet you." She dialed Paola's number and asked her to meet by the fountain in the park where the pigeons were. "Frank, you're in for a treat. Paola is about the most beautiful woman you'll ever meet. She's my partner in this affair, very brave, very discreet. You'll probably fall in love with her. Most men do." He didn't respond. His mind was solely on Celia.

They crossed the wide driveway in front of the hotel and walked to the far end of the park where few people ventured. A sharp wind slashed their faces with sand. "Tell me what you can about all this before she joins us," Frank asked.

She looked around her. No one was near. "Paola is my best agent, a highly paid escort. One night she gets picked up at the bar by an Arab named Hassan Al Kidwa."

He laughed, interrupting her. "A real charmer, the king of the swindlers."

"You know him?" she asked, incredulously.

He told her what he knew about Al Kidwa.

"Paola needs to hear this," she said, stopping him from saying more.

She gave him the briefest outline of what had been going on: the phone call Paola overheard, their turning to Ratner, the information she got on the Khaybar Brigades from her CIA contact, Al Kidwa's reaction to the news of General Rashid's death, and the video of the theft of a nuclear bomb in Pakistan.

He knew all about that now, though he had not yet actually seen the complete video. There had been no way to avoid the subject once he got to the airport. News of the hijacking and snippets from the video were playing on all the television monitors throughout the terminal and screamed from head-lines in every newspaper and on the covers of special editions of magazines. Images of mushroom clouds were everywhere. It was all anyone talked about. He had grabbed every article he could find and read each carefully on the plane. He began asking her for every word she heard from Chaim Ratner and the questions her CIA contact asked when a tall brunette in spike heels and a tight-fitting brown silk dress walked directly towards them.

Celia introduced them to each other. She watched them carefully as they shook hands and smiled at each other, but neither of them revealed any reaction. They were both profes-sionals. They sat on a bench alone in the middle of a large grassy meadow by a pond. No one else was in the park. Gusts of wind prickled like needles against their skin, but at least it felt safe to talk there. Frank interrogated Paola in minute detail, wanting to know exactly what Al Kidwa said, when had he switched from Urdu to Arabic, how had he acted on their second meeting, how many lines of coke had he laid out, did he pay her in dollars, dirhams or euros, was the TV on when she entered or had he turned it on, had he screamed when he had his orgasm?

When he finished interrogating them both, he stood up and paced for a moment in silence. He came back and stared intently at each of them as if searching for some clue. "It stinks," he said finally. "It all feels off to me. Hassan Al Kidwa may be a whore." He paused for a second, realizing his mistake, then continued. "But he's a damn good one. He doesn't make moves that aren't calculated. I simply can't imagine him letting a stranger overhear a conversation that important."

Paola nodded. She had always felt like Hassan was acting that night. "But why?" she asked.

"Well, that's the big question, isn't it?" he said. "From what I've seen of him, his only motivation is money. If he were part of this plot, he might want to make his importance known to sell information, just as you did. Or, perhaps he only got wind of it and pretended to be involved to be first to market with what he knew."

Celia and Paola looked at each other with questioning eyes.

"But there's a much bigger question, I think," Frank asked. "Why did these terrorists put out a video in the first place? No one released a video before 9/11. The Japanese didn't produce a film of coming attractions before Pearl Harbor. Why such a warning?" he paused thinking. "They haven't made any demands like 'remove all American troops from Afghanistan or we'll blow up Kabul.' Maybe they still will, but that hasn't been the MO for terrorist groups lately from the little I've heard. They tend to blow things up and brag about it afterwards."

"Except for hostages," Celia added. "They could hold a whole city hostage and get a billion dollars in ransom money."

"They could," said Frank, "but if I had a bomb like that, I'd be more tempted to use it. It's a reasonable hypothesis, though."

"I think it's all psychological," added Paola. "The whole point of terrorism is to create terror, to scare your enemy. The threat of a nuclear bomb going off may spread more fear than the effects from one that has exploded, however horrible that might be. Right now, the whole world is in a panic because we don't know if the bomb will end up in Islamabad, New York or Tokyo. Once it goes off it will be a huge tragedy, but something finite. For now, they have succeeded in terrorizing the whole world."

Frank looked at Paola with renewed respect. *She may be as smart as she is beautiful,* he thought. His eyes met Celia's, nodding slightly to acknowledge how impressed he was.

"There's a third possibility," added Frank. "Even if they plan to use it, they might want to prove their ownership by releasing this video. No one ever heard of this Khaybar Brigade before now, just like no one had heard of the Islamic State before they suddenly overran Raqqa and Ramadi and challenged Al Qaeda for leadership in the global jihad. If this Khaybar Brigade blows up some city, they will be the king of the mountain and everyone will know it was them. Yet my instincts tell me this is a military or intelligence operation from some state, maybe India or Afghanistan, or even Pakistan itself."

"Or maybe the United States," added Paola, surprising them both.

"Yes," said Frank, "It could be any of them. It's awfully sophisticated, whoever is behind it. Hassan Al Kidwa may or may not be part of this plot, but he's all we got. Whatever Ratner promised you, you can be sure he is watching Al Kidwa like a hawk. Hassan won't be able to sneeze without Ratner knowing. I think it's much more likely Al Kidwa's using Paola as a conduit than anything else. I suspect he'll try to sell something through you. Be careful though, this could get dangerous. You'll be expendable to him. Has he contacted you again?"

"No," said Paola, "but he will."

Chapter 24

The yellow school bus pulled up to a rusting corrugated steel warehouse on the outskirts of Port Qasim. None of the streets were paved in this dilapidated part of town and many of the surrounding buildings appeared abandoned, their windows largely boarded or broken. Except for a few stray dogs, the area looked uninhabited. The mujahideen in the cars following poured out and took up positions around the warehouse. The front shutters opened and the bus pulled inside. Four men in white lab coats unhinged the case in the rear of the bus and removed the gleaming container with the care of a midwife delivering a child. They lifted it onto the deck of a speedboat mounted on a trailer and then placed it in a container built into its hull.

As it turned twilight, the door of the warehouse opened with a clattering sound and the speedboat was backed out, towed by a black SUV. The mujahideen piled back in their cars and followed the trailer and boat as it meandered its way down dirt roads to a launching dock at the western end of the port far away from the commercial fishing boats and trawlers whose lights were just coming on. The boat glided off the aluminum trailer and gently entered the dark waters with barely a sound. In minutes its motors roared to life and the boat sped away. A merchant vessel flying the flag of The Netherlands and carrying a load of rice waited ten minutes offshore. Customs agents and soldiers equipped with Geiger counters and radiological detection devices had already searched the freighter in its berth before it left port, but the vessel was now in international waters when the speedboat pulled alongside it. A hoist on the freighter lifted up its prize, which was then stowed safely in a secret storage space below deck as the speedboat returned to port and the freighter sailed away into the darkening sky.

Chapter 25

Paola left Frank and Celia in the park and took a cab to her apartment. After soaking in a hot salt bath, she lay in her bathrobe on a soft brown leather recliner and looked out at the last rays of sunset. She held a bowl of warmed up spinach lasagna in her lap. Her thoughts were of her mother and little brothers in Brazil. They couldn't possibly imagine what her life was like now. For them, prostitutes were mostly losers hanging on street corners servicing johns in cars for the price of a fix. She glanced at the modern oil painting hanging over her gas fireplace. It had cost her more than her father had earned in his lifetime. She had sent the family money, but her father had forbidden her mother from accepting anything from her. It hurt her deeply. She took a sip of white wine from a glass on the table next to her. Her cell phone vibrated, startling her.

She read the text, from Hassan. "I need to see you right away. Can you please meet me in front of the Starbucks in the Marina? It's urgent."

She replied with a smiley face, but her own wore a frown. Her stomach hurt. Her throat tightened. She wished she had never stumbled into this affair. But part of her was also proud. She knew he'd call her again and he had. She threw on a black dress and pulled on tall boots, sat before her vanity and quickly applied some makeup. She texted Celia and left her apartment. She wondered what could be so urgent and why he wanted to meet like this. A welcomed cool breeze greeted her as she waited outside for her Uber driver to arrive. She felt more elated than afraid. It was game on.

At the Starbucks she ordered a latte and took a seat at a table outside. A moment later a black Mercedes pulled up and Hassan stepped out and beckoned for her to join him. He hadn't shaved and his clothes were wrinkled, but he smiled at the sight of her. "Come in, please," he said, holding the door for her. He slipped in beside her and they drove off into a sea of headlights.

"What's wrong?" she asked.

"Nothing, nothing," he said. He seemed nervous though, but tried to hide it. "Nothing to worry about. I need to go out of town for a couple of days, that's all, and I didn't want you to think I had forgotten you."

"You could have told me that on the phone," she said. "What's going on?"

"I was expecting a visitor to arrive, but for some reason he never showed up and now I have to fly to Tehran to meet him. It's business, you know." He shrugged. "You do what you have to do."

"How long will you be gone?" she asked.

"Just a couple days. But honestly, I am disappointed. I was looking forward to spending time here with you." He looked at her and smiled mischievously. Even though he hadn't shaved, he smelled of after shave. He reached into his pocket and removed a small wrapped package. "I wanted to give this to you."

She looked at him suspiciously. He smiled mischievously. "What is it?" she asked.

"Please open it." It was a jewelry box. Inside was a zirconium teardrop necklace. "To match your earrings," he said.

"It's beautiful," she said.

"Here, try it on."

She handed him the necklace and faced away. He clasped it behind her. The pendant was exactly the right length for her dress. She reached over and kissed him. His breath was sweet as usual. "You are so kind, Hassan" she said. "Thank you."

"It's nothing."

Her mind raced ahead trying to figure out what all this meant and what she might get out of this encounter. She badly didn't want to lose contact with him. They were in a bubble passing silently through crowds out in the cool evening air. "I've never been to Iran," she improvised. "Why don't I join you?" She paused for a moment. "I won't even charge you."

He studied her. "You flatter me. That may be an offer I can't refuse. But I'm not sure there'd be time to go back to your flat to get your passport."

She smiled. "I was in this situation once before," she said. "I had the chance to meet the Sultan of Brunei at his palace, but I didn't have my passport. I promised myself I'd never let that happen again." She reached into her red patent leather purse and pulled it out.

He stared at her a long time trying to decide what to do. "You know it's everyman's fantasy to have his beautiful escort want him for himself, not for his money."

"And the same is true for us, probably more so," she said. "You didn't have to give me this necklace, I realize. Thank you."

"It is my pleasure." He took out his cell phone and spoke Arabic to someone, arranging her ticket and a visa.

She pretended not to understand. She knew his phone was being bugged so Celia would learn where they were going, even if she were unable to call before she left.

He turned to her. "Everything will be arranged. I would love to have you come with me. You will need to wear a hijab, I'm afraid. There is much about this affair that we'll need to hide. We can stop on the way to the airport and get you one. We can buy you any other clothes you need when we get there. You'll enjoy Tehran. Do you ski?"

She laughed. "No, but I would love to be your date."

As they drove to the airport, Chaim Ratner received word that the target was on the move, flying off to Tehran with Paola in tow. He picked up the phone and called Major General Mordechai Lonzman, head of Military Intelligence. "Mort, the girl is going with him. I assume your boys are in place?"

"We've got it covered," General Lonzman replied. "So far so good. Even Hansel and Gretel couldn't have left a better trail."

"A lot could still go wrong," Ratner reminded him.

"It always does," said Lonzman.

Chapter 26

Celia and Frank stayed in the park for a long time after Paola left, catching up on each other's lives. Frank had little to recount, his days changing only with the seasons. But Celia was eager to hear his descriptions of the land and the animals and especially of Simba. It really didn't matter what he talked about, she realized. She liked hearing his voice. Celia's stories were mostly about business.

"And what about your private life?" Frank asked, a question whose answer he had long feared might demolish his dreams. Frank lived in the moment. He didn't have plans or hopes for the future, but he had nurtured his feelings for Celia for two years. Along with Joanna, she was a constant presence in his life. *I'm a bigamist,* he joked to himself. *I love both women.* But Joanna was dead and Celia, so long departed, was now sitting in front of him, all flesh and bones, especially flesh. He had worried that he had idealized her, was afraid that he wouldn't even recognize her. As soon as he had seen her though, he knew immediately his feelings were real. It was like coming home. All of his off switches were turned on. His heart beat too fast. His stomach was full of nerves.

"I don't have much of a private life," she answered. "I mostly keep to myself. I've dated a few guys, but nothing serious. The men here aren't very interesting. They're vainer than women. Everything's superficial. To be honest, I've been missing Cuba a lot. The people there are real, even if they're poor. Here, money is the judge of everything and it's so boring. My goal is to save enough of it to buy a small cottage in the south of France, as you once advised me to do, I recall. I'd be happy spending all my time gardening and eating baguettes and cheese. I'd become a big fatty and be completely at peace."

Frank smiled, trying not to reveal the level of relief he felt that she had not found anyone. He searched her face to see if there were any sign of feelings for him. But she was inscrutable. Behind the façade though, Celia hid her own desires. If she had fallen for the idea of Frank before, she now wanted the reality. She wanted his protection, to have those pure blue eyes see only her, to feel his hands on her. She wanted him, all of him. It felt like the first time she had wanted a man so physically. She had admired the way he lived his life, his artistry, his idealism, the way he held himself. She loved to watch him walk and work. But now she wanted him up close, wanted to hold him and be taken by him.

She showed none of this, nor did he. They were old friends, colleagues now, professionals. The world was teetering on the edge of a nuclear disaster and they held the only slim lead. They must not fuck up. They could not let their personal desires get in the way of their judgment. They mustn't take their eyes off the job at hand. Celia felt unqualified to handle this burden without Frank's help. She depended on him. And the more Frank felt his love for Celia grow, the more he thought of Joanna and the more terrified he became. He couldn't let anything bad happen to Celia. He had failed to protect Joanna. He couldn't fail again. Try as hard as he might to suppress his feelings for her, though, the core of him roared under the surface for him to sweep her off her feet like Tarzan and swing through the forest to safety.

They walked into the glittering lobby of the hotel where Celia lived in a vacuum sealed from the desert storms outside. The whole country was artificial, thought Frank. Celia wanted him close by her even though Hassan also stayed at the same place and had met Frank before, as she had just learned. But Hassan rarely ventured from his room and the Lebanese surveillance team, which she never caught a glimpse of, would warn her if he came near. They rode up in awkward silence on the elevator like strangers. Frank's room was on the same floor as hers. The key card connected with its comforting clicks and they walked into the foyer of his room.

As he closed the door behind them, they both let out their breath. They stood staring at each other like two awkward school kids not saying a word. But their eyes spoke. He saw the same frightened desire that she did. Alarm bells were ringing in his ears. He could not let any harm come to her. But his desire, he knew, was greater than even his fear.

She had not known till this moment the full extent of her love for this man. She trusted him completely, but had left him in solitude with his grief, for two long years. He had never reached out to her. Her infatuation, she had told herself, was a childish fantasy. She took a step forward before she realized what she was doing. Tears welled in his eyes. They stood a half-foot away from each other saying nothing when suddenly the phone rang, a terrible electronic sound that shattered the silence.

She pulled it from her pocket. "I have to get it. It's Paola." She read the text out loud, "Off to Tehran."

Frank closed his eyes. "That changes everything," he said.

Chapter 27

Ilan stood up from the beach and stretched. He had been scribbling notes since breakfast and it was already past lunch. The sun was overhead and the sand too hot for bare feet. He stood at the water's edge and kicked off his sandals.

"Go 'head in," said Frank. "I'll join you."

They both stripped and dove into the cool water. When they came out they sat on some rocks to dry before retreating to a patch of shade. Ilan picked up his recorder and turned it back on.

"So, where were we?" asked Frank.

"You told me about Hassan Al Kidwa and Chaim Ratner and how Paola went with Hassan to Tehran. What happened there? You said that changed things. How so?"

Frank looked up, searching his memory. "We were getting almost real time intelligence from the Israelis, courtesy of Chaim Ratner. He shared everything with us, more than I would have expected from him. Once in Tehran, Hassan went by himself to meet with some private funders, people who had supported various plots he'd orchestrated over the years, mostly gun runners. The really important piece of information was that he had a half hour meeting with Qasem Soleimani, the commander of the Quds Force. Qasem is a hard man to meet, so this was significant. It seemed to indicate that the Iranians were involved in some way in this plot. It would explain the military-like planning of the operation, but it would also raise a lot of questions about the destination of the bomb and its purpose."

"Ratner sold the information for a huge fee to the Saudis. I contacted some old friends in Riyahd. Like everyone else, they were preoccupied by the loose nuke, but news of Hassan's meeting focused their attention on Tehran. In the millennial Sunni-Shiite conflict, an apocalyptic weapon in the hands of its archrival posed an existential threat to the House of Saud. It had worked hard and spent billions to prevent the Iranians from developing a bomb. When the Americans blocked Israeli plans to bomb Iran's nuclear facilities, something the Saudis had fervently prayed for, they settled for a fifteen-year agreement to freeze sensitive nuclear activity in exchange for a halt to Western sanctions. It wasn't the deal Riyadh wanted, but it gained them time. Now, in an apparent Hail Mary pass, Iran may have gotten its bomb anyway by simply stealing one from Pakistan."

The shadow of a large bird passed over Ilan and Frank. Ilan looked up. It was the blue heron, lumbering up river, honking as if appearing to struggle with excess baggage.

"What, if anything, did Paola learn?" asked Ilan.

"One very important, curious thing, actually. Though she never accompanied Hassan to any of his meetings, she managed to get him drunk one night. It was forbidden to have any alcohol, but Hassan managed somehow to have an endless supply delivered to his hotel room. Paola used an old prostitute's trick: if you eat a stick of butter first, you won't get drunk no matter how much alcohol you consume. So, she challenged Hassan to a drinking duel, downing shots of Tequila. When he was thoroughly soused, she got him to talk about General Rashid's suicide. She saw how genuinely upset he had been when they had watched the first TV news reports. If anything could get him to open up, she thought it might be this."

"And did it?" asked Ilan.

"It did. He cried when she asked about it, said that Akram Rashid was like a father to him, that Rashid would never commit suicide. He said he had arranged for his wife to get an operation at a hospital in Israel, the only place in the world that performed the procedure, he claimed. He was proud of that. When Paola asked how he had arranged such a thing, he said it was through the former head of Mossad whom he sometimes did business with, Chaim Ratner."

"Chaim Ratner?" exclaimed Ilan.

"The very one."

"What did this mean? What did you do with this information?"

"We learned about this when Paola returned to Abu Dhabi. Luckily, I had suggested the three of us meet privately before Paola debriefed Ratner. She came directly from the airport, met us at Celia's lawyer's office, so we were pretty sure no one was listening in. Of course, we didn't share any of this with

Ratner when he came in a half hour later. I knew how deceitful he could be. I even suspected he may have been behind the attempt to kill me in Beirut years before when I was negotiating with the PLO for Al Haig. So, I didn't trust him. But now there were a million questions swirling in my mind."

"Like?"

"Like why hadn't Ratner told Celia about his relationship with Hassan and their roles in helping General Rashid's wife? What was the quid pro quo Hassan and Ratner got for treating her? And, what was behind Rashid's death? Was he killed to shut him up?"

Ilan interrupted. "So, what was Hassan's role? Was it to cast blame on the Iranians? It seemed he may have purposefully leaked information about the plot to Paola. But why?"

Frank smiled. "The simplest answer was that Hassan and General Rashid were involved in carrying out an Iranian plot and Hassan was making money doing some insider trading. But I'm always suspicious of simple answers. Besides, that still doesn't explain why Ratner would withhold such important information from us and from everyone else?"

"So, what did you do?"

"I had a hunch that we should interview Rashid's wife in Tel Aviv. "

Ilan's stomach growled. He was starving, but didn't want to do anything to interrupt Frank's story. "So, you went to Israel?"

"Yes, right after our meeting. Celia came with me. Paola remained in Abu Dhabi in case Hassan asked to see her. We went straight to the hospital in Tel Aviv and were taken to her room, alone with Rashid's wife and a translator. She was a beautiful old woman with long silvery hair that fanned out across her pillows. She appeared to have recovered well from the procedure and told us she would be returning to Lahore in a couple weeks. She credited her surgeon, Dr. Carlston, for saving her life. After offering our condolences for her husband's death, we asked when she had last spoken to him."

"It was the night before they found his body," she said. She didn't believe it was a suicide. Her husband wouldn't do that, she was certain. He loved life too much. He was very upset on the phone though, she said, more than she had ever heard him before. He couldn't stop talking about not being able to protect 'his boys' who had been gunned down.

"I asked her what exactly he had said, what were his words?"

"'He said it was all his fault. He had been tricked. He said he had done something because he loved me. I didn't understand what he meant by that.'"

But Frank added, "I thought maybe I did."

Chapter 28

Frank and I were at my lawyer's office when Paola informed us that Chaim Ratner had helped Hassan get General Rashid's wife into a Tel Aviv hospital. Frank coming back into my life had turned me inside out. Finding out that Chaim Ratner, the partner I turned to for help, was hiding vital information from us and may have been involved with Hassan Al Kidwa, made me want to throw up. Things were moving too fast. I didn't know what to believe anymore. I was afraid I had put Paola in real danger. We hardly had time to digest Paola's news when Ratner showed up.

We went through the charade of that meeting, not letting on what we had just learned. As we were leaving, out of earshot, Frank suggested we fly to Israel to meet with General Rashid's wife, hoping she might shed light on her husband's involvement. Our passports, he said, would be enough to get us tourist visas. In the taxi to the airport Frank passed me a note warning me not to discuss anything for fear the taxi might have been bugged!

We rode in silence. When we got inside the terminal, he pulled me aside and we found a corner in a hallway where we could be alone.

"What the fuck!" I exclaimed. "Ratner's using us!"

Frank agreed. He thought the whole thing with Hassan had been a setup from the beginning. Hassan had been the bait and Paola the unwitting conduit of whatever information they wanted the world to believe. By being the first to identify the Khaybar Brigades, Ratner gained credibility as the only person with any inside window on the plot. But we now knew that Ratner, Hassan and General Rashid had all been engaged with each other before the bomb had been stolen. That was no coincidence. Clearly, they were all somehow involved in the plot.

But why? What was he up to? Why would an Israeli help a jihadi terrorist organization steal a nuclear weapon? Did he send Hassan to Tehran to shift attention to the Iranians? All our assumptions had been turned upside down. "Maybe Ratner's planning to intercept the bomb, blame Iran and give the Israelis the pretext to destroy Iran's nuclear plants," I suggested.

"That makes a lot of sense," said Frank. "It would also force the world to take the security of Pakistan's nuclear arsenal more seriously and make Israel the hero of the day. It was brilliant, but far riskier than anything Ratner was known to engineer in the past. What if he lost control of things?"

We flew to Tel Aviv and met with General Rashid's wife. We never learned what Ratner got in exchange for helping her. But she said her husband told her he had been deceived. By whom? By Ratner? Hassan? The terrorists? Did Ratner kill

Rashid to silence him? Or, did something go wrong and Rashid, feeling he had been deceived, commit suicide?

There were too many questions with no answers. Everything pointed to Ratner being at the center of the plot and using Paola and me to leak whatever information he wanted. But we didn't know that for sure and we didn't have any idea where this was all headed. What could we do? I again argued that we should just take ourselves out of the equation. Pack up and go back to the farm. At least we wouldn't make things worse. But Frank said it was too late for that. He thought we had to stay engaged with our eyes wide open. But I felt like we were way out of our depth.

I convinced Frank to call Washington, to share with them what we knew. "I'll call Jill," he said, "Jill Samuelson, the National Security Advisor. She was Joanna's roommate at Yale and her best friend. We never spoke after Joanna was killed. But she'll listen to me. We were very close."

Once in Tel Aviv, we took a cab to the American Embassy and used a secure phone to call Jill's personal mobile. She picked up on the first ring. I listened in.

"Jill, this is Frank, Frank Reynolds." There was a long pause.

"Hi, Frank. I wondered whether I'd ever hear from you again, though I've been hearing a lot about you the last two days," Jill said with her well-known sarcasm. "I tried hard to find you after Joanna's death, but you disappeared without a trace."

"Yeah. I'm sorry I never called."

"Well, I'm just glad you're alive. You sound like your old self."

"And congratulations, by the way," Frank said. "You finally got NSA, the job you always wanted."

She laughed. "Condolences would be more appropriate. Frank, I was surprised and confused, to say the least, to learn you surfaced in the middle of this crisis. You can explain everything later, but it's real helpful to have someone on the ground I can trust. What do you know?"

"Jill, we're all being taken for a ride, but where it's going I can't tell you. You remember Chaim Ratner?"

"The Mossad chief who tried to get you killed in Lebanon, I recall. He seems to be back running this show in Israel."

"Yes," Frank added, "but he may have been running things all along, in Pakistan, too. We just learned he did General Rashid a big favor months before the bomb was hijacked, got his wife a life-saving operation in Tel Aviv. I'm pretty sure he set us up with Hassan Al Kidwa."

"Us?" Jill interrupted.

"Celia Ramirez is a source I developed in Cuba." He stopped and glanced at me standing by him. "She worked with us before Joanna's death. We're good friends. I'd trust her with my life. Celia employs a group of prostitutes to collect intelligence, worked with Ratner before. We think Ratner planted Hassan with one of her working girls, then purposefully leaked the name of the Khaybar Brigade. Got everyone's attention, then sent Hassan to Iran to meet with General Soleimani. I think it's a ruse to make everyone think the Iranians are behind this."

He could hear Jill breathing through her nose. "We've been studying your friend, Celia. We've got PhD theses being written about Celia Ramirez right now. There are even some analysts at Langley speculating that this might all be a Cuban plot. We've got every available team trying to figure this thing out. We did learn that Ratner called General Rashid shortly after the story broke about the attack, but we don't know what they discussed. The call was encrypted. We asked him. He didn't deny it, claimed he called to get whatever information he could from the officer in charge of the airbase."

"Did he say anything about helping Rashid's wife get an operation in Tel Aviv?" Frank asked.

"No. That's new. Quite disturbing." There was a moment's pause. "Once we learned that Hassan met with Soleimani, the working assumption around here has been that this is a Quds Force operation, a cheap way for them to get the bomb. But this news about Ratner and Hassan could change things. Let's say you're right and Ratner was involved somehow. What's his game?"

"Your guess is as good as mine."

"Frank, this is very helpful, but it's going to be a hard sell. I can't walk into the Oval Office and advise the President to trust the security of the world to the impressions of a prostitute in Abu Dhabi. I need more than that. Maybe Iran is behind this. Maybe Hassan is a link between Soleimani and the Khaybar Brigade and Ms. Ramirez's prostitute actually stumbled across some vital information. Maybe Ratner simply did a favor for General Rashid and then called him for information after he heard about the theft at Sarghoda. That all seems a lot more plausible than some theory I just heard from a former CIA agent who disappeared eight years ago about some convoluted plot to steal a nuclear bomb in Pakistan that is being run by a former Israeli head of Mossad who uses a prostitute spy ring in Abu Dhabi to divert attention to Iran."

There was a long silence. "Jill, I knew you'd understand."

"Frank, believe me, I do. I'd never underestimate you. I just need more than this."

Chapter 29

Piled high with sacks of rice, the rusted grey freighter sailed up the Gulf of Aden into the Red Sea, joined a convoy of 40 ships headed north on the Suez Canal and turned east at Port Said into the Mediterranean, destined for the Carmel Terminal at the Port of Haifa. Gliding by a giant aircraft carrier belonging to the U.S. Navy's Sixth Fleet, the crew of the Dutch-flagged freighter smiled nervously to each other. It was dawn when the ship finally docked. Seagulls squawked overhead.

Having filed the requisite International Ship Security Plan and receiving an entry permit, the captain of the vessel waited to greet the loading master and his two boarding crew. They knew each other by first names. The procedures were routine. He handed them three crew lists, seaman's papers and passports for immigration control. Ten minutes later a port security team boarded to check for compliance with the International Ship and Port Facility Security Code. Everything appeared in order.

Because of the high-level alert in place since the Sarghoda attack three weeks earlier, a special unit of elite Mossad counter-terrorism experts came on board to inspect the hold. Their usual group leader, Colonel Waxman, had been called away to another assignment and, in his place, Major General Mordechai Lonzman, head of the Military Intelligence Directorate, led the search operation himself. The officers, five men and one woman, had never met Lonzman before and were duly impressed by his hands-on management style. They carefully examined the cargo, the sleeping quarters and engine rooms, but were steered clear of the secret compartment in the hull of the ship.

After all the customs, immigration and security agents departed and only the loading master remained on board, the crew removed the heavy metal flooring in the hull and carefully extracted the shiny silver football in its crate. A white van pulled alongside the ship and five men lowered the crate to the dock with a small crane and lifted it into the rear of the van. Followed by a black sedan, they drove to the end of the wharf, navigating around the labyrinth of concrete barriers, and stopped to show their papers. All were in order. The gate lifted and both vehicles exited into the traffic on Kef Krayot Street and then turned onto Route 6, Yitzhak Rabin Highway, in the direction of Jerusalem.

None of the men spoke. An hour and a half later they saw in the distance the glistening gold Dome of the Rock next to the Al-Aqsa Mosque, the third holiest site in Islam, which dominated the skyline of the old city. The men in the van prayed silently. Jerusalem was the city of their dreams, almost on a par with heaven itself. It represented the sum of all the humiliations their families had endured for centuries and their hopes for eternal redemption. The mosque was situated in the center of the Temple Mount, the holiest site in Judaism where the Jewish First and Second Temples once stood, the epicenter of the millennial Arab-Israeli conflict.

The van drove into the old city through Zion Gate and inched its way to Ha Nostrim Street by the Church of the Holy Sepulcher. On the surface little had changed in the centuries since Jesus walked on the same cobblestone street, where he was crucified, buried and resurrected. It was here in the 2nd century AD that Emperor Hadrian built a temple dedicated to the Roman goddess Venus in order to bury the cave in which Jesus was interred. Later, the first Christian Emperor, Constantine the Great, replaced the temple with a church.

The rotunda, which contained the remains of a rock-cut room, thought to be the burial site of Jesus, was undergoing an archeological restoration and was closed to the public when the five men descended carrying their crate. They were dressed like ordinary workmen. The room smelled of dust and incense. Alone in the rotunda, the men removed a marble sheath beneath a large window well, exposing a secret stairwell cut into the limestone that led to a cavernous basement deep underground. All of them were veterans of many battles, but as they carried their parcel down a ladder, they shuttered with the fear of God.

An hour later a messenger arrived at Hassan Al-Kidwa's hotel in Abu Dhabi. After making eye contact in the lobby, Hassan stood up and walked to the men's room followed by the young man. Alone at the urinals, the men whispered to each other, then left in their separate directions. Hassan stood in a corner of the lobby and called Paola.

"Good morning, my princess. I hope I didn't wake you."

"Not at all," she said. "I just came in from my run."

"You are a better man than me. It is a glorious day, is it not? A momentous day. I have taken the liberty of ordering us brunch in my room. I hope you will join me. I have a special present to give you."

Paola thought for a moment before answering and was surprised to hear herself say, "My handsome lover, I'm sorry, but I can't come over right now. I have an appointment with my hair stylist in ten minutes. He's very jealous of my time. I mustn't disappoint him." She had not planned to say this, but she was tired of being used. Maybe some pushback would throw new light on the situation, she thought. There was a long silence on the other end.

"I'm afraid this can't wait," he said with some annoyance.

"That's exactly what Leon, my hairdresser, told me," she laughed.

"Paola, my dear. This is quite serious. We are both realistic business people, you and I. This is a matter of great urgency. A deal must be made and there is only a small window of opportunity. I'm sure you'll understand."

"I don't. I don't understand anything anymore," she pushed harder. She knew her phone was tapped and wondered what those listening thought. What would Celia think?

"I will explain everything when you get here." He exhaled loudly. "Maybe it is time to bring your friend Celia here with you."

Bastard! She thought. *He's been playing us all along.* The curtain had lifted. He was calling her bluff. "What do you want, Hassan?" she asked, searching for a way to be in control. She wanted to tear his eyes out.

"I want you to convey a message, an important offer. It's as simple as that. Your friends will pay you handsomely."

"I don't need the money."

"Perhaps not, but this is bigger than both of us. You know that. Come as soon as you can, immediately. There is no time to waste. Call Celia."

She did as she was told. Celia was waiting for her in the lobby. Frank was at the Saudi consulate, meeting with some former colleagues now in charge of the kingdom's intelligence agency, the General Services Directorate. He begged Celia not to go without him, but she and Paola felt they shouldn't wait.

"He's dangerous, Celia. You two know too much."

She assured him that nothing would happen to them, that Hassan was probably the most watched person on earth right now. She understood Frank's fears. Celia and Paola rode the elevator to Hassan's floor holding hands. Neither of them knew what to expect. Hassan opened the door and they walked in, glancing around.

"It's OK. We're alone," he said. He held his hand to his heart and bowed slightly to Celia. "It is an honor to meet you finally." She did not answer, but nodded her head slightly.

Paola spoke. "You used us."

"You were well paid. You were only doing your job."

"The whole thing was an act, then," Paola said with some bitterness.

"Not all of it, actually. But now there is no longer any reason to pretend, so let us get down to business. Every minute counts. My friends in the Khaybar Brigades have employed me to convey certain messages to you. They have succeeded in placing the missing nuclear warhead in Jerusalem, God be praised." Celia gasped. "They have a simple proposition to make to the Israelis, which you will be kind enough to deliver when you leave here. Begin evacuating all the Jews from the city in 12 hours, by midnight tonight, and nothing will happen. If not, my associates will turn it to ashes."

"What about all the Palestinians?" exclaimed Celia.

Hassan smiled. "They will live peacefully. With their nuclear deterrence, there will be no more occupation. No more harassment. They will pray at Al-Aqsa without hindrance. They will live like a normal country with freedom and dignity. If the Israelis refuse or try to come back, the Palestinians will have the honor to die as martyrs, to ascend to heaven from the place where Mohammed did."

"It's suicide," exclaimed Paola.

"We have had many brave suicide bombers; many martyrs have preceded them."

"It's murder," said Celia.

"Call it what you wish." He looked at his watch. "There is very little time to act. I will be leaving here, but will be in touch with you. Remember this number 078421. It is the first sequence in the permissive action link. The Pakistanis can verify that that is correct. My associates are arming the bomb as we speak. It is set to explode at precisely 12 midnight tonight, God willing." He opened the door and showed them out.

Deep underground below the tomb of Jesus the six mujahideen cautiously uncrated the bomb, placed it on the floor in front of them and prayed. Theirs would be the greatest martyrdom ever. They would rise to heaven by the noble sanctuary where Mohammed had ascended on a horse. They thought of their loved ones whom they hadn't seen in months or years. They evaluated their lives. Their names would be revered for centuries to come. Some thought of the 72 dark-eyed virgins who would greet them; others of meeting Mohammed himself. The engineer among them sat cross-legged before the shining oblong device and placed his hands on it, as if expecting to feel its pulse. He looked at his watch: 11:59:30. Then he entered a series of coded signals unlocking the permissive action links. Immediately, a red light began to flash. Next to that a digital clock counted down the hours, minutes and seconds left. A switch could reset the timer, but a single finger on the trigger was all it would take now to turn the holiest of cities into a burning inferno.

Chapter 30

Frank was coming in through the front doors of the hotel out of breath as Celia and Paola hurried through the lobby. The Saudi Consulate was just a mile away and he had run the whole way. His shirt was soaked. "Thank God you're safe," he said.

"Let's cross to the park," Celia suggested. The hot desert air smacked them as they exited. They hurried across the parking lot and a six-lane boulevard and strode into the lavish green oasis of the park. It was cooler there, but they were in the open and presumably could be overheard by a directional listening device. Frank took out his phone and turned on some music.

"What happened?" he asked.

"He dropped any pretense," Paola started. "He told us he was working for the Khaybar Brigades; said they had placed the bomb in Jerusalem and would detonate it at midnight tonight, if all the Jews didn't evacuate the city."

"Jerusalem! Holy shit!" said Frank. "It's the Apocalypse!" A feeling of dread surged through him, the same feeling he felt when he heard his car explode with Joanna inside.

For a moment, none of them could speak. "Maybe we've been wrong about Ratner," Celia said finally. "Maybe Hassan knew we were working with him, just like he knew Paola was working with me, and he threw us off track by letting us know that Ratner helped him get General Rashid's wife into the hospital. Ratner may be a shit, but he wouldn't want to threaten all the Jews in Jerusalem, would he?"

"I don't know," Frank thought out loud. "The connection between the three of them—Hassan, Ratner and Rashid—couldn't be a mere coincidence. But maybe there's more going on here than we can figure. The Saudis are convinced this is all an Iranian plot, as you'd expect. They shared with me a piece of evidence they got from Pakistan. Apparently, there was one fingerprint found at the scene of the attack at Sarghoda. It was traced to a retired Iranian Quds Force commander who had fought in the Iran-Iraq war. The CIA is crunching the data as we speak. I don't know what to make of it, but I'm suspicious."

Celia interrupted. "Look, we could speculate all day long, but we need to let the Israelis know what we just learned. There's not much time."

"You're right," Frank said. "Call Ratner. I'll call Jill."

When Celia reached Ratner, he told her to stay where she was and not do anything until he could reach the Prime Minister. Five minutes later he called to say the Prime Minister wanted to hear from them directly. A car picked them up a few minutes later and whisked them to the U.S. Consulate. Although relations between the UAE and Israel were good—Israel selling Abu Dhabi a billion dollars' worth of surveillance cameras, electronic fences and sensors to monitor strategic infrastructure and oil fields each year—there were no official relations and Israel had no embassy of its own. Rushed through security, they were ushered into a windowless room in the basement for a videoconference with Israel's Security Cabinet. Chaim Ratner was also there. Everyone was just taking their seats when the Prime Minister walked in and they all stood.

"Let's get started," the Prime Minister said. He looked into the monitor across from him and addressed Celia, Paola and Frank. "Thank you for coming and for the work you've been doing."

He nodded to Major General Lonzman who proceeded to question them about what had just happened in the hotel room. They briefly recounted what Hassan had told them about the deadline and the group's demands. They had 11 hours left.

The Prime Minister, clearly exasperated, asked how they could be sure the bomb was in Israel? How would they know Hassan spoke for the terrorists?

Frank answered. "Sir, Al-Kidwa was the first to lead us to the Khaybar Brigades, before everything came down. That's not proof, I realize. But if the Pakistanis validate the permissive action link sequence he gave us, that means he's directly connected and presumably can speak for them."

"It would also mean they have a live bomb," the Prime Minister noted, ruefully, in his deep baritone voice.

"Sir?" General Lonzman, interjected, glancing at his phone. "We just got confirmation. The sequence is real."

Everyone looked anxiously at each other. The atmosphere was corrosive. Finally, Efrom Berg, in charge of Israel's strategic forces, asked Paola directly. "You were in Tehran with this man?"

"Yes, sir."

"Did you meet anyone else?"

"No, Hassan left several times. We ate some meals in restaurants. That's all."

"Did he speak about the Iranians or give you any hint why he was there?"

"No, not at all."

Berg closed his eyes tightly and strummed his fingers on the table. "I think we must proceed on the assumption that this is an Iranian attack. We should act just as we would if a warhead were delivered on top of a missile."

The Prime Minister cut him off. "Efrom, please. Let us say good-bye to our guests before we debate among ourselves what to do."

He turned to face the monitor again. ""Miss Ramirez, how did you leave things with Mr. Al-Kidwa. How can we communicate with this so-called Khaybar Brigade?"

"He said he would contact me."

"No way to reach him?"

"I don't think so."

Chaim Ratner spoke up. "Al-Kidwa left the hotel right after Celia and Paola. We tracked him to his car and then another. He's trying to evade us. He left his cell phone in the hotel."

David Hoffman

The Prime Minister turned again to Celia, Paola and Frank, "Before you leave now, is there anything you've seen or heard that makes you doubt in any way whether this threat is real?" Celia and Paola shook their heads. "Nothing that would suggest Iranian involvement?" Again, they shook their heads.

"Thank you for everything you've done. We are very grateful. Continue to liaise with Mr. Ratner. If you think of anything else, don't hesitate to let him know."

"May I say something before we go?" It was Frank. All heads turned to the monitor. "If I may, I just spoke with the head of Saudi intelligence. They have evidence, a fingerprint taken from the scene of the attack that belongs to a former Quds Force officer. Everything points to Iran, except for one thing. You have deterrence, plenty of it. I know the Iranians very well. I was there during the revolution. They may be religious fanatics, but they're in no way suicidal. They would never do this."

The Prime Minister thanked them again and the screen in the consulate went blank. Frank had been cut off before he had a chance to say what he knew about Ratner, *but perhaps that news will best be delivered by Jill,* he thought.

Inside the Security Council the mood turned dark. Chaim Ratner countered what Frank had just said, arguing that deterrence wouldn't necessarily dissuade the Iranians in these circumstances. "They believe there wouldn't be enough evidence for Israel to retaliate. They will claim this is the work of some fanatical terrorists. But let us not forget that this so-called Khaybar Brigade took its name from the battle that expelled all the Jews, where Shiites believe Mohammed designated Ali as his successor. This is their creation myth. This is Iran through and through."

Efrom Berg looked to the Prime Minister. "We should give Iran an ultimatum."

"Yes, of course," he interrupted, "But what do we do in the meantime?"

Lonzman spoke up. "We should begin an orderly withdrawal. Our top priority must be the safety of our citizens."

At the other end of the conference table General Pelletier raised his voice, "Don't do it. We would be giving them a victory. It would create panic. The people expect us to protect them, not to order an evacuation at the first sign of a threat. We must stay strong. We are descendants of the heroes of Masada, don't forget."

"An unfortunate example," the Prime Minister quipped with an ironic smile. "Everyone at Masada killed themselves. But your point is well taken. We should not do anything to show weakness or cause panic."

David Ben Cohen, the head of Shin Beth said, "I agree, wholeheartedly, but we should deploy the army to search every inch of the city for the bomb. Discreetly, of course."

Lonzman responded, "Discreetly? Deploy the army in a massive dragnet for a nuclear bomb discreetly? Good luck."

"So, we do nothing?" Lonzman asked.

"We wait," said the Prime Minister and, after a pause, "And we pray."

Chapter 31

We all looked at each other in stunned silence after the screen went blank. None of us spoke. An American marine came in and asked if we would stay for a few minutes, as the Consul General wanted to speak with us before we left. He offered us water, but we politely refused.

The room was covered in white soundproofing material with fluorescent lights overhead and had an operating room feel to it. I think we all assumed that others were watching or listening to us, so we made awkward small talk. After fifteen minutes the Consul General walked in with a short, trim man dressed in khakis and a white short-sleeved shirt who was introduced to us as the Israeli Prime Minister's Chief of Staff. He thanked us for our "exceptional patriotism." None of us corrected him.

With a grim face, he told us that the Israeli Security Cabinet was preparing to evacuate Israelis from Jerusalem. Given the mood in the Security Cabinet, I doubted that was true. If Hassan Al-Kidwa called again, he said, we were to inform him that the evacuation would begin by 6pm. Also, given the time pressure, Paola should urge Mr. Al-Kidwa to open direct negotiations with him, the Prime Minister's personal representative, which could commence immediately. Al-Kidwa's safety was assured. He asked that we repeat this message, which Paola did verbatim, without hesitation. I could see the man's hand shaking as he offered it to each of us with his "gravest appreciation."

A car was waiting for us as we were escorted to an interior courtyard, but Frank suggested we walk instead. It was now the middle of the afternoon. We walked past the British Consulate down the road and turned along the marina where there was a slight breeze. A couple blocks away from the consulate we finally let out our breaths and talked. I could tell that Frank was excited to be back in the game at the highest levels; but having grown up among government officials, I was less impressed. Whatever was going to happen would happen and there was little any of us could do except serve as a conduit of messages. If we had been players in this drama before, we no longer were. The feeling of being used depressed me. It conjured up old feelings about Jose.

Walking felt good. I badly wanted to hold Frank's hand, but I knew I shouldn't. After fifteen minutes or so we hailed a passing taxi and drove back to the Etihad Towers. Pressed against Frank in the back seat, I looked at him carefully as he stared out the window. The lines around his eyes had deepened since our time on the farm. He had a familiar, earthy smell. I was glad we were quiet so I could take the time to study him. My heart fully opened to him. When we got to the hotel we went up to my room to wait and used our time to go ever every twist and turn in the story. I could tell that Paola was getting increasingly angry as she realized the extent of Hassan's deception. Finally, she left to go to her apartment and promised to call the moment she heard from Al-Kidwa. She knew exactly what to say. There was no room for improvisation.

I brought Frank an iced tea and sat beside him on the couch. "I miss Simba," he said.

"Do you? I thought you were kind of enjoying yourself in this game."

He smiled. "I really don't. I guess part of me still likes the adrenaline rush. I'm glad I had a chance to say my piece. Maybe it will make them pause a moment before they blow the Iranians to smithereens," he said.

"God, I hope that doesn't happen," I replied.

"But a much bigger part of me wishes I were back on the farm. This is madness here, this whole make-believe city. The world's gone crazy, killing people for sport. What could Hassan be thinking? He's no terrorist. He's not motivated by hatred, only by money."

"And women," I added.

"Someone's obviously paying him handsomely. But who? I don't think the Iranians would ever risk this. It could be Al Qaeda or ISIS, but neither of them has claimed credit for the Khaybar Brigades. The whole thing feels stage-managed to me. We're all being used as pawns in someone's play. So, yeah, I miss Simba terribly. I wish we were home listening to the birds and the river instead of sitting here in the air conditioning above this desert of concrete. And you?"

"I'd give anything to be there right now," I admitted. Inside me, though, all I could think about was how much I loved this man. I wanted him, on the beach by the river or right here on this couch. He was the one thing I could totally count on. I wanted his protection. I wanted him to take me from this insanity. "I'm scared here, Frank. This whole affair is surreal, like Alice and Wonderland meets Hieronymus Bosch. I don't know what would have happened to us, if you didn't come out. Thank you for coming here."

He didn't say anything, just stared at me intensely. Frank's blue eyes were like a pool of water drawing me closer. Finally, he said, "Celia, when this is over, will you come back with me?"

I had so badly wanted to hear him ask me this. I felt my stomach turn inside out. I opened my mouth to answer, but nothing came out. He moved closer to me, reached up with his other hand and stroked my hair, my eyes drowning in his. I leaned forward and felt his lips touch mine. We kissed long and slowly. When I opened my eyes, his were on me with a look of wonder. His hands explored me like a blind man, tenderly, savoring the moment. I wanted him faster, wanted him to tear my clothes off. He took his time, this mountain man who whittled model boats. When his hand went between my legs, I moaned and bit his ear. He lifted me off the couch and carried me to my bed and we made love in waves of ecstasy.

Frank's phone ringing woke us from our reverie. He fumbled in his pants pockets to find it. It was Jill. He sat on the edge of the bed with his back to me. She asked him to be her representative in Jerusalem. She didn't leave him any space to consider. He would have access to the Prime Minister and other top officials. There was a plane that left Abu Dhabi secretly for Tel Aviv via Jordan twice a week, she told him. It was used for high-level trade in the security sector. There was one leaving in two hours, a Geneva-based private airline PrivatAir, an Airbus A319 registered with the tail-number D-APTA. They were sending a helicopter to his hotel. It would be there in twenty minutes. He was to proceed directly to the command center under the Knesset and report to her.

"I'm coming with you," I said.

"You can't. You need to stay here with Paola. I'll be alright."

"What about the bomb?" I pleaded. I felt like a sharp blade had cut me in half. "Don't go, Frank. Let someone else do it."

He smiled and his blue eyes melted me again. "I'll be careful. You too. Don't do anything foolish with Al-Kidwa. He's dangerous and you know too much. Promise me."

I promised him. We held each other and something inside me told me it was the last time I would see Frank.

Chapter 32

At 2pm, shortly after the Security Cabinet meeting ended, the Prime Minister went on national television to announce that an Israeli officer, Mordecai Levy, was missing from his unit based in the Golan Heights. A photograph of the young man appeared on the screen, but no other information was provided to protect his privacy. A nation-wide manhunt was launched. "No stone will be left unturned," said a grim-faced Prime Minister. "We have no reason to believe he has left our territory. For the time being our search will concentrate on the greater Jerusalem area, where we believe he is being held. We are treating this as a terrorist act. To aid in our search, I am immediately calling up all available reserve forces."

The terse announcement shocked the country. Journalists demanding more information came up against an unprecedented wall of silence from the usual sources. Only a handful of officials seemed to have any knowledge of the details of the alleged kidnapping. Reporters were told that Levy's family was sequestered at an army base in the Negev. The total lack of information heightened the sense of crisis. The Prime Minister's expression told of an even greater drama than what his words conveyed. People who had lived through wars and bombings were left feeling uncommonly confused and insecure. It was as if as if the whole country held its collective breath in anticipation of the worst.

The streets of Jerusalem were quickly filled with the sounds of sirens and the urgency of military patrols that had been told to look for possible hiding places. Soldiers were ordered to report any suspicious activity and to be especially careful of hidden explosive devices. They were ordered to move with the greatest possible speed. At a command center run in the basement of the Knesset, General Lonzman checked off each box on a grid of the city as patrols swept them for any signs of the missing soldier. Meanwhile, a fleet of black vans equipped with highly sensitive radiological monitors discreetly traversed every street in Jerusalem. On television there were frantic scenes of soldiers and reservists being deployed, of uniformed military and police forcing entry into the homes of Palestinians in the Old City and surrounding neighborhoods. With no hard information, journalists were left to speculate on which faction was behind the kidnapping. But none took credit.

In Tehran, through the intersession of the Egyptian Ambassador, a secret meeting was arranged between Gadi Eizenkoh, Chief of the Israeli General Staff and General Mohammad Ali Jafari, the Commander of the Iranian Revolutionary Guards. They met on a small island off the western coast of Lebanon, both officers arriving by helicopter. The meeting lasted only a few minutes, the men forced to shout above the screech of the helicopter turbines. The Israeli formally notified Iran that it would be held responsible for any nuclear incident, accusing Iran of being responsible for the theft of the missing Pakistani bomb. General Jafari denied his side had anything at all to do "with this contemptuous terrorist act" and pledged his country's help in finding the real perpetrators.

"Someone is manipulating you," he said, staring without blinking at his Israeli counterpart. "We would never harm Al Quds," using the Arabic name for the city of Jerusalem. "A notorious Jordanian arms dealer recently tried to sell us this bomb for a billion dollars. We turned him down," he said, before heading to his helicopter. He stopped at the steps, turned and yelled to the Israeli, "Make him a better offer."

In Abu Dhabi, Hassan Al-Kidwa managed to evade the two-dozen Mossad surveillance teams that followed him by car, motorcycle and on foot. It hadn't been easy. He rushed through streets and shopping malls and downtown crowds and in and out of three different vehicles; but Mossad's drones never lost sight of him until he entered a house that had been prepared with a tunnel that exited a block away. Arriving at his destination around 4pm, he paused to look up and down the empty street before entering the grey single-story safe house. A young armed man greeted him respectfully. "I'm black," Hassan told him.

Hassan moved to the refrigerator, which mercifully had been stocked with cold beers, as he had instructed. He removed his suit jacket and loosened his tie. Rushing about Abu Dhabi had worn him out. When he finally caught his breath, he dialed Paola's number on a phone the young guard handed him. She answered on the first ring. "Hello, my dear," he said. "I must be brief. Please tell your friends that they can signal their acceptance of our demand by announcing plans to evacuate the Jewish settlement of Modi'in in the West Bank in accordance with UN Resolutions. Then, if they complete the withdrawal before midnight, we will give them another 12 hours to evacuate the remaining illegal settlements." She quickly repeated the message she was instructed to say before he abruptly hung up, took the SIM card from the phone and broke it in half.

Paola called Celia and Frank and they reported her conversation to Chaim Ratner. His men had lost track of Al-Kidwa, he told them, and there was now no way to contact him. It was vital to find a way to do that. He put them on hold for a minute to take a call from General Eizenkoh's helicopter. "Paola," he said when he got back on, "if Hassan calls again, tell him money is no object. We will pay any reasonable price to resolve this issue."

Around the same time a new video began circulating on the web from the Khaybar Brigades. Ominously, it began with a stock photo of the Dome of the Rock and the same monotone voice in English counting down from ten. At zero the screen went white with the sound of an explosion, growing ever louder as a dark mushroom cloud rose like an angel of death into the sky. "Infidels, the moment of your destruction is at hand. In the name of Allah, the most merciful, the most compassionate, we condemn you to eternal hell. No longer shall you rape our women, steal our land or desecrate our holy shrines. You, kuffar, who fear death, prepare to burn. We who fight in the name of Allah, know that paradise awaits those who give our lives for Jihad. Our holy martyrs are prepared to enter the garden of paradise. Praise be Allah."

Chapter 33

At a quarter to five, General Eizenkoh's helicopter landed on the helipad between the Rose Garden and the Knesset. The Prime Minister was waiting for him in a secure room in the operational command center with General Lonzman and Chaim Ratner. The massive manhunt so far had failed to turn up a single clue. The Prime Minister was chain smoking, a habit he thought he had beat a week before. His eyes were a deep purple. His skin looked ashen. He was fuming. "What have we got?" he asked.

"Jafari denied everything of course, but I made it clear we would hold them responsible and respond in kind," said Eizenkoh. "He insists money is at the heart of it."

"There's a new video, Gadi," said the Prime Minister. "It doesn't say the bomb is here, but it would take an idiot not to infer it was."

"How can we be sure it is?" asked the Chief of the General Staff.

General Lonzman answered, "I'm afraid it's pretty certain. I personally inspected every ship coming from Pakistan and found nothing. But after the threat from Al-Kidwa, I had our men go back a second time with Geiger counters and go over every inch. An hour ago, they found small traces of radiation on a Dutch freighter that came from the Port of Qasim. Together with the valid permissive action link sequence Al-Kidwa gave us, we conclude the threat is real. We've taken the captain into custody. The crew is missing. I hope to get descriptions of the men very soon."

The PM paced around the room trailed by a cloud of smoke. He looked at his watch. 5pm. 7 hours left.

General Eizenkoh, glared at Ratner. "Chaim says Al-Kidwa got away. We trailed him to a safe house, but, apparently, he escaped through a tunnel. How do we communicate with him, if we can't find him?" General Eizenkoh asked him.

"I think he will contact the girl."

Eizenkoh, exasperated, asked, "Can someone tell me why the fuck we are communicating through this prostitute? How did this happen? Why would Al-Kidwa set things up this way? Everything else about this operation seems so sophisticated."

Lonzman answered. "It's perplexing. We think he saw an opportunity, after discovering that the girl had exposed him."

Ratner added, "Al-Kidwa's a real opportunist. I think he's in this for the money. He didn't have the means or the experience to organize this operation himself. His patrons, whoever they are, bought his services. But being Al-Kidwa, he tried to sell the bomb to Iran for a higher price and got rebuffed."

General Eizenkoh interrupted, "Or, he was going to his masters for instructions."

"Perhaps, Gadi. In either case, the girl offered a convenient way to communicate with us. So be it. She can give him our answer and he can see facts on the ground."

"Answer to what?" asked Eizenkoh.

"Al Kidwa contacted the girl again and said they'd give us another 12 hours, if we evacuate Modi'in by the midnight deadline," Ratner explained. He spread his hands in front of him. "At least they're bargaining. They could just pull the trigger, but this feels more like the opening of negotiations. Maybe Jafari is right. Maybe it will come down to the price we're willing to pay."

"That's precisely the question I keep asking myself," said the PM.

"And what is your answer, if I may ask?" General Eizenkoh replied.

The Prime Minister crushed his cigarette into an ashtray on the conference table and lit another, paced back and forth a few steps and responded, "We will never abandon Jerusalem, not even temporarily." He tapped his fist on the table. "That is a given. They must know that. That is not negotiable. So, if they are bargaining, they may believe we can be forced to give up something less—Modi'in and the other West Bank settlements, for example. Asking us to evacuate Modi'in as a starter, makes me think they are realistic, very practical. Otherwise, they'd just blow us up without warning. They know we're not leaving here. Their ultimate goal may be to regain the pre-'48 boundaries, as every government in the world demands of us."

"But where would they stop?" asked General Lonzman.

"Once they got Modi'in and the other settlements, they'll demand we evacuate East Jerusalem. We'd be under tremendous pressure from the international community to concede. The Security Council would pass another fucking resolution demanding both sides compromise in the interests of peace. It's fucking absurd."

"Surreal," said General Lonzman. "Maybe we should pretend to give them Modi'in to gain time. They won't be able to keep this bomb hidden forever."

"Yeah, but how long can we keep the bomb secret?" asked the PM. "We've been lucky so far that it hasn't leaked. The Levy charade has worked better than we could have expected, but it's only a matter of time before some investigative journalist or hacker discovers the truth."

General Lonzman nodded in agreement. "With this latest video," he said, "they've all but announced its location and purpose. If we evacuate the settlements in the face of this threat, it will create absolute panic and everyone will leave the city. Any rational person would." *That's only half the city,* he thought to himself.

"Mort," General Eizenkoh responded to Lonzman, "If the Levy kidnapping is discovered to be a ruse and our citizens learn that their Prime Minister has lied to them, we won't have any credibility left to manage anything. It's worked so far, but how do we keep people's trust in the hours and days ahead, if there are days?"

"We find him," said Lonzman.

"What?" asked the PM.

"We declare victory. We announce that our soldiers discovered Levy and killed all the kidnappers."

"How do we do that?"

"We anticipated this problem from the outset. How to bring an end to this fiction? We deployed a unit of Shin Beth to stage the kidnapping. As far as Sergeant Levy is concerned, he was actually kidnapped by some radical Palestinians. He can recount his story to the news media. It will make you look like a hero, sir. You'll have all the credibility in the world to lead us through the next stage."

"So, what do I do? Go on television and announce our brave soldiers have rescued Mordecai Levy and, by the way, we now have another problem, a nuclear bomb in our capital?"

They were all silent. Finally, the Prime Minister spoke again. "We have three problems as I see it: finding the bomb, answering the terrorists and managing our own people." He looked again at his watch. "As of now, we have the next six and a half hours to locate the bomb. If we're to win more time, we'll need to begin evacuating the 60,000 residents of Modi'in right away. The terrorists have all but announced the bomb is here in Jerusalem. We mustn't let them control the agenda. If we want to maintain people's trust and manage this situation without panic, we'll have to get out in front of this. We can't just rescue Levy and call off the search. Any announcement about his release must be coupled with an announcement about the bomb. We can claim the two events are somehow related."

"Sir?" Chaim Ratner stood up and banged his fist on the table. "I've got an idea." They all turned to look at him. "We rescued Sergeant Levy in Ramallah or Nablus. But in doing so, we discovered plans to detonate a dirty bomb in one of the West Bank settlements using radioactive uranium from the stolen Pakistani warhead. For everyone's protection, we launch a massive campaign to evacuate the entire West Bank—Jews and Palestinians alike. We make ourselves the defenders of the Palestinian people against these Islamic fanatics. Of course, as part of this, we also evacuate Modi'in and the other settlements to protect our own people."

General Lonzman stood up and pumped his fist in the air. "Chaim, I take back anything bad I've ever said about you. This is brilliant."

"How long would it take to clear the whole West Bank?" General Eizenkoh, asked.

Lonzman answered, "We could probably do it by noon tomorrow. We'd need the extra twelve hours they promised, though, for sure."

"But will Al-Kidwa think this is a concession?" General Eizenkoh asked again. "Or, will he feel he's been tricked?"

Ratner answered him. "We tell him we agree to his demand in exchange for his offer of more time and he'll see we are complying. He knows he's got us between a rock and a hard place. I think he'll appreciate our ingenuity in evacuating the whole of the West Bank, but he'll think he's winning the game. Meanwhile, we do everything humanly possible to find and dismantle this bomb."

They all nodded their approval. This could work. It all depended on ultimately finding the bomb.

"One more thing," Ratner spoke, still standing. "In the end it will be more important than anything." His intensity was frightening. "Once we clear out the West Bank and evacuate all the Palestinians across the Jordan River, there should be no coming back. We turn this satanic plot on its head. We use this threat of a nuclear bomb to liberate Judea and Samaria forever."

No one could speak. The enormity and finality of his plan shocked them, but it offered a way out, a way to turn tragedy into opportunity. The Prime Minister nodded his approval, turned and left without a word.

Chapter 34

Hassan Al-Kidwa sat glued to his television, nervously eating pistachios, dropping the shells on the floor in an-ever growing pile beside him. The Prime Minister's address was just ending, broadcast live on Al Jazeera. It was just before six pm. His tone and expression were grave. There was defiance in his words and his eyes glared with anger.

"These psychopathic killers will stop at nothing to spread their ideology of hatred. They will not spare even their own people. They think they can frighten us to leave our land, which God has promised us. They will not succeed. We will crush the hands of those who threaten us as well as their backers."

The Prime Minister continued. "We have a high degree of confidence that this so-called dirty bomb is located in the West Bank, waiting to target one of our settlements. Depending on the wind, radiation can spread across the entirety of the West Bank. To protect everyone from any harmful radiation that could be released, I am ordering the temporary evacuation of all Jewish settlements and Palestinian villages and neighborhoods in the West Bank, starting with Modi'in Illit and the neighboring towns. We will proceed in an orderly fashion. Every effort will be made to locate and dismantle this dirty bomb and return everyone to their homes as quickly as possible."

"Palestinian residents shall be relocated across the Jordan River, as agreed to by the government of Jordan, and all Israeli citizens will be provided accommodations at designated facilities in Tel Aviv. Everyone should be careful to bring their identity papers and other vital documents with them. No one will be allowed to remain. The military will patrol all population centers to prevent looting. Any civilians found in these areas will be arrested and removed. This is an unprecedented emergency evacuation involving up to 3 million people. No interference with the authorities will be tolerated. But be assured, just as we rescued Corporal Levy moments ago, so will we neutralize this threat. We have lived through wars and terrorist attacks before. Our strength and our unity will keep us safe. God bless you all."

There was no hiding the shock on the faces of the commentators who spoke after the Prime Minister's address. Reactions from people on the streets were hysterical. Cyberspace lit up with frightened, apocalyptic messages. Within minutes, streets and highways were clogged with cars. Convoys of military vehicles streamed in an opposite direction from those fleeing the West Bank. The Palestinian Authority denounced the incursion of Israeli military forces into their territory and called for an emergency meeting of the Security Council. But any protests were drowned out by the sheer magnitude of the operation, as tens of thousands of soldiers rolled into the West Bank in a seemingly endless river of steel.

There was panic in Modi'in Illit as military police swept through the apartment complexes amidst the blare of air raid sirens. Television crews were ubiquitous. When settlers resisted, they were forcibly handcuffed and led into waiting vans. It seemed everyone was shouting. Mothers carried screaming babies. Terrified residents grabbed their most precious belongings. Many men and teenagers carried weapons with them as they boarded buses for safer ground.

In the Palestinian areas there was chaos and resistance. The military used tear gas and stun grenades to try to control the crowds. Sit-downs and protest marches were met with force and demonstrators who refused to move were herded with electric cattle prods onto buses. Shots rang out, but there was no organized paramilitary defense. The Palestinian police mostly stood aside or cooperated to establish some sort of order. But pandemonium reigned. Helicopters filled the sky. Fear and loathing prevailed in every alleyway and street. Shouts of "Allahu Akbar" rose like a chorus from the maddened crowds.

All of these scenes streamed continuously on social media and tv sets around the globe. World leaders denounced the terrorists, but refused to criticize the Israeli response. "What else could be done?" most commentators asked. The United States and other nations offered equipment to help search for the radiological device and began a hurried repatriation of their nationals. Although Jerusalem itself was not designated for evacuation, many of its residents, mostly from the Jewish quarters, packed their belongings and drove to stay with friends and family further removed from the West Bank. A bunker mentality spread across the holiest of cities.

After watching scenes of the evacuation from Modi'in, Hassan Al-Kidwa smiled with satisfaction. He phoned Paola again and told her he was extending the deadline to noon Tuesday, presuming the withdrawal from Modi'in was completed by midnight. All other settlements in the West Bank would have to be emptied by noon tomorrow. After that, he would negotiate. She tried to say something about money, but he hung up before she could finish. He then called a number in Jordan that was automatically rerouted through three other numbers in Israel before connecting to the mujahideen seated around the bomb in the sub-basement of the Church of the Holy Sepulcher. "They have begun the evacuation of the Jewish settlement. We will give them another 12 hours, until noon tomorrow, to clear the others. Reset the timer. God willing, we will prevail."

Amidst the chaos on the ground and the diplomatic and media fury swirling around them, the Israeli Security Cabinet met and authorized the arming of a half dozen low yield nuclear warheads that were loaded onto six F-16I *Sufas* outfitted with extra fuel tanks. The cabinet issued an urgent and formal request to the U.S. President to provide mid-air refueling for an attack that would target Iranian military facilities. At an underground strategic air command post at the Nevatim airbase on the edge of the Negev desert, pilots from the 116th squadron went over their flight plans, which had become significantly more challenging given the lack of surprise. Iran's air defense forces had been put on the highest state of alert.

Sitting in a circle on the dirt floor in the sub-basement of the church, six war-hardened fighters argued in sharp whispers about the news from the social media chatter that was their only source of information of events cascading above them. Light from their few candles flickered off the ancient limestone walls. Their initial elation after hearing that the Prime Minister had ordered the evacuation of the first Israeli settlement, Modi'in Illit, had given way to anger and frustration over subsequent reports of mayhem and violence against Palestinians in the territories.

"We've been tricked," said one of the older mujahideen who had a scar that ran from his ear to his mouth and was missing several fingers on one hand. Another cursed Hassan Al-Kidwa whom they were pledged to obey. A respected Pakistani Taliban commander in the tribal areas of North Waziristan had recruited them, but they had never met the urbane Al-Kidwa. They had no reason to trust him. But these were seasoned, disciplined soldiers who were trained to take orders. Still, they could not ignore the fact that Israeli soldiers were forcibly deporting Palestinians across the Jordan River. This was a calamity demanding a shift in their strategy.

Using the secure encrypted system that had been established, they called Al Kidwa in Abu Dhabi. Keeping to protocol, they kept the conversation to less than thirty seconds. The engineer, the most senior member of the team, told Al-Kidwa that they refused to extend the deadline. "The Jews are using us," he told him, "trying to turn the tables in their favor. We are ready for martyrdom, not games." Al-Kidwa argued, but to no avail. The men would not budge: twelve midnight, not a second later.

Chapter 35

Emerging from the elevator on the ground floor of the parliament, the Prime Minister, trailed by a half-dozen aides, walked through the open glass doors to a small parking lot at the rear of the building and ducked into his car. He wanted to be alone to think for a while, he told his aides. His chauffeur drove him the ten minutes to his house in a leafy neighborhood of Jerusalem with a security detail in front and behind his armored plated car. He was weary. Despite a massive hunt for the bomb, the army hadn't uncovered a single lead. The forced evacuation of Palestinians disturbed him, reminding him of the stories he was told growing up of the forced deportations of his relatives from Poland and the herding of Jews into the camps. He mistrusted Chaim Ratner, felt a visceral repulsion around him; but the ex-Mossad chief seemed to grasp the situation better than anyone else.

He looked at his watch. It was 7:19 pm, less than five hours before the original deadline. Thank God they had gotten another twelve hours, if indeed they did. 'What would I do, if we didn't get that extension?' he asked himself. Despite the coolness of the air conditioning, he was sweating freely. He thought of his kids safely ensconced at U.S. universities. They had wanted to come back to be with him during the crisis, but that was out of the question. He wished there was some excuse he could use to get his wife away from the city, out of harm's way; but that was simply impossible. They both knew their fates were intertwined. *It would be a quick death at least,* he realized. He would not want to be alive to witness the aftermath.

His wife greeted him at the door wearing an apron. The house smelled of fresh bread and meat. She'd cooked him a brisket, she told him, his favorite dish. She helped him out of his jacket. His underarms were soaked. She had seen him through many crises, even the death of an infant son, but this was different. He had the frightened look of a man about to die. He held her tightly, squeezing her as if he could not let go. They had been together for forty years, raised two children, buried a son and their parents, overcame their infidelities and won some bitter political campaigns. It all seemed to be coming down to this one moment.

He swore a million times, swore to himself, truly believed that he would never surrender Jerusalem. But was he committing the sin of pride? Did he have the right to deny his people the truth, to let them decide for themselves? The stolen warhead was a much larger bomb than the one that razed Hiroshima. So many would die. So many would suffer horrible burns and slow death from radiation poisoning. He was acutely aware of the effects. There was still time to evacuate the city, he realized. Yet it was unimaginable that Jerusalem could be destroyed.

Everything he believed in, everything he worshipped, his friends, his history, they were all part of this holy city. It would be an abomination. But there had been nothing but ever-more horrendous abominations. This terrorism was a cancer that continued metastasizing and growing ever more monstrous.

"Shaina, I'm afraid," he admitted.

She pulled her head back to examine him. The sadness in his eyes was unfathomable.

"Why do they hate us so?" he asked. "Was it not enough to kill six million of us in ovens? And now they want to burn another million here in the land of our ancestors? We swore we would never allow this to happen to us again. We would be stronger than our enemies. Will it never stop?" He was shaking with anger and fatigue. "I have just given the order to bomb Iran, if this thing explodes; though I am not at all sure they are the ones to blame. We have no choice, but to show we will not go meekly to the ovens again. If we go down, we will take them with us. There will be a price to pay. An eye for an eye, blood for blood." He paused. "But it is pure madness."

She could feel him crying softly. Her mind flashed on their son who died and how he cried in fluttering breaths against her chest. "What about the Palestinians?" she asked. "Why would they kill their own people?"

He pulled back and wiped his eyes with his sleeve. "They believe there is no higher glory than martyrdom. It's an apocalyptic hallucination, difficult for us to understand." He registered the fear on his wife's face. "Shaina, I love you so dearly. I should send you away somewhere safe, but I can't. It wouldn't be right. You understand that, don't you?" She nodded her head. "I have failed to protect you and failed to protect our people." He hung his head in shame.

At a far corner of Ben Gurion airport, the roar of the Airbus A319's engines fell silent and stairs rolled into place. Frank bounded down the steps. A black Mercedes was waiting for him on the tarmac and rushed him at high speed to the command center in Jerusalem. He was given security badges that would allow him to go anywhere and was briefed on the search operation and the evacuation underway in the West Bank. So much had happened since he left Celia's apartment. He had not seen the new video, nor heard the announcement about the rescue of the kidnapped soldier, and the Prime Minister's dramatic address to the nation about a dirty bomb and the order to clear the West Bank.

General Lonzman briefed him about the offer to extend the deadline by twelve hours, if all the residents of the Modi'in settlement were evacuated before midnight. Nothing was said about the ruse to forcibly evacuate the Palestinian territories, but Frank understood it immediately. They were trying to establish some kind of deterrence. Lonzman recounted General Eizenkoh's meeting with the Iranian, General Jafari, and told Frank they were preparing to respond in kind.

At 8:30 pm, the Prime Minister returned from home. Frank introduced himself as the White House's liaison. It was understood that he had a direct line to the National Security Advisor and, therefore, could respond faster than even the Ambassador. The PM thanked him for his help and then ducked into a private briefing. Frank noticed a message on his phone from Celia to call her. She had found a letter in her mailbox from General Akram's wife that had probably been sitting there for days. It said that she had received something from her husband that they needed to see. It didn't explain what it was about. She wrote that they were moving her from the Sourasky Medical Center in Tel Aviv to the Hadassah hospital in Jerusalem. Given there was little else to do in the command center, Frank decided to visit her and see what she had.

The Mercedes was waiting to take him. The Hadassah hospital was only 6 miles away; but the road, route 386, was filled with cars piled high with people's belongings moving slowly away from Jerusalem. His driver turned on his siren, which merged with all the other sirens that pierced the evening air. They got to the hospital in twenty minutes. He stopped at the front desk and flashed his badge. A male nurse in a blue smock took him running to her room two stories above them. She looked to be sleeping, but sat up at the sound of his voice. He suddenly realized he was without an interpreter. He exchanged pleasantries with her in Urdu, using the three or four phrases he recalled from his time as an analyst studying Pakistan's nuclear development.

"You speak Urdu?" remarked the nurse with evident surprise. Frank turned and now noticed the man's fine features and silky black hair.

"You're Pakistani?" he asked.

"I am," said the young man with some pride.

"Thank God," Frank uttered to himself.

She handed Frank a letter, which she kept under her pillow.

"What's it say?" asked Frank, passing it to the nurse.

"It says he was tricked by the Israeli. He didn't realize what would happen. Why would they kill so many of his men for something that was," he stopped in mid-sentence, tapping his forehead. "Khota jiali, khota jiali?"

Finally, he raised his index finger. "It means counterfeit."

"What else does it say," asked Frank.

"It's mostly about his devotion to her, how much he loves her, how happy he was that he could get her the operation she needed. But he says he traded the Israeli something that was worthless. He couldn't live anymore with the blood of his men on his hands. He prayed she would understand."

Frank put his hand on his heart and bowed slightly to the nurse, thanking him. "You'll never know how important this is." Then he reached over and kissed Akram's wife on both cheeks. "May I keep this for one day?" he asked while the nurse translated. She smiled broadly and gave him her blessing.

He went running down the steps and into the Mercedes. But just as he was about to call Jill, his phone rang. It was Celia.

Hassan had called again, she said. His men refused to obey him anymore. The deal was off. They would explode the bomb at midnight. Hassan offered to tell them where the jihadis were hiding, where the bomb was, but only if the Israelis delivered 5 million euros in unmarked, non-consecutive bills and deposited 95 million in an account he'd give them. She called Ratner, though, of course he had already intercepted the call.

He was extremely upset, but said they'd get the money together as soon as possible.

She pleaded with Frank to leave Jerusalem. "There's nothing you can do anymore."

"Oh, but there is," he said, and dialed Jill.

Chapter 36

Paola and I sat watching the television screen in her apartment in silence. Neither of us dared give voice to the terrifying fear that gripped us. The live, round-the-clock coverage from Jerusalem could be interrupted at any second, we knew, by the death flash of a nuclear explosion. At one point the screen flickered and went blank for a moment and we both screamed, but it was just a wobbling satellite or a solar flare or God knows what. After that, we turned the sound down and began to talk.

Paola made tea. "I'd give anything for Frank to get the hell out of there," I said.

"You really love him, don't you?"

"I do. I think it's the first time in my life I loved someone so deeply. With my husband, Jose, it was all a superficial infatuation. He had charisma, charm and dashing good looks and he moved on the dance floor like he was born there, but it was all just surface stuff. I didn't know the real person. We had good sex, but were never really intimate. Do you know what I mean?"

Paola laughed, which relieved some of the tension. "Are you kidding? That's my life's story. I've never known real love. The longest relationship I had was when I was twelve years old with the boy in the shack next to ours. We never did anything, but I was sure we would marry. His family moved away one night and I didn't even have the chance to say goodbye."

"How sad," I said. I told her how Frank and I had lived together in paradise without ever consummating our love, which I now know was always there between us. He was still grieving the loss of his wife and neither of us realized the other was open to having a romantic relationship. In a way I'm glad it happened that way. We were friends first. I told Paola about our love making that afternoon before the National Security Advisor asked him to go to Jerusalem. He couldn't really refuse Jill, I suppose, but I will always blame myself for letting him go.

My eyes glanced at the scene of Palestinian families boarding buses in Ramallah. "What are you going to do after this when it's all over?" I asked Paola, wanting to change the subject from Frank.

"I've been thinking a lot about that," she said. "I've decided to get out of the 'business'. I don't regret what I've done. It allowed me to escape the favela, see the world and have some financial security. But I'm done with it. I've had it with always faking it, pretending to be someone I'm not. It makes everything else in my life phony. I just want to be the girl I was before all this. Men come on to me all the time, but they don't see the real me. Sometimes I fantasize I'll meet a blind man who will love me because of my voice and the things I say, not my beauty. I've been blessed and cursed with this face."

"What will you do instead?" I asked.

"Whatever it is, it will be simple and it won't make any use of how I might look. I might even go to school. Believe it or not, I'm fascinated by foreign affairs and, I suppose, I now can claim some experience."

"Don't become a spy though," I teased her. "The stress is not worth it."

"I won't. Believe it or not, I've always wanted to be a welder. I hear they make good money. And what about you, Celia?" she asked me. "What are you going to do when this inevitably ends."

"I guess it all depends on how it ends. Frank asked me to go back with him and live on the farm. I'd love that more than anything in the world. But whatever happens I'm finished here. I had a good run. I have plenty of money. I've often dreamed of buying a little house in the south of France, maybe near some lavender fields and an old castle, and raise rabbits and vegetables. I kidded Frank that I would grow fat on baguettes and Brie. Doesn't that sound delightful?"

"It does," she laughed. She stood up and went into the kitchen and came back with some Camembert and white wine. "It's all I could find," she explained. It felt good to laugh.

Suddenly Paola's phone rang. It was Chaim Ratner. He told her they'd have the cash together by 9:30 pm. If Hassan called, she should follow his instructions. I never realized till that moment that they might expect Paola to make the delivery.

Of course, I'd go with her. I couldn't let her go alone. I knew Frank wouldn't approve, but I would do anything to help find the bomb and save him. Sure enough, Hassan called a short time later and Paola told him she'd have the cash. At 9:20 pm there was a knock at the door and two men in immaculate white dishdasha and keffiyas stood holding two leather flight bags. They introduced themselves as officials of the Emirates Central Bank, asked our names and had us sign a receipt. It was as easy as ordering a pizza. The bags they left us were filled with neat stacks of 500 Euro notes.

At 9:30 pm, precisely, Hassan called. He told us we both had to come with the money, that we must not bring our cell phones and warned whoever was listening that he would not reveal the location of the bomb, if we were followed. He had ways of knowing. A white SUV would pick them up by the lobby. "Leave now," he said.

Downstairs the car was waiting for us with its rear door open. We climbed in. He nodded and pulled into the traffic. I watched behind us, but could see no obvious tail. They'd have to be following, though, I thought. After ten minutes we pulled into an underground parking garage and were led to another car and asked politely to put our heads down on the seat. The driver emptied the contents of the two bags into a duffel bag and passed some kind of wand-like device over the money. Satisfied, he waited several minutes and then exited.

By 10 pm we arrived at our destination, a single-story brick villa with an attached garage. A stone-faced young man with a Kalashnikov opened the door. He patted us down and waved another wand, like the one in the car, around us to detect any transmissions. Hassan was seated on a green divan, but rose with a large grin to greet us. "Welcome," he said and went to kiss Paola on her cheek, but she turned her head away.

"Time is in short supply, so let us forego pleasantries and get the business out of the way," he said. He looked through the cash, fanning the bills like a card shark and opened his computer. He sent instructions for the bank transfer, waited thirty seconds for confirmation of the deposit and exclaimed, "Hamdu'Allah!" In an instant the funds were redirected to a dozen other banks and forty other accounts with an algorithm he had perfected from years in the arms trade.

"We need to go," he said.

"What about the location?" I demanded.

"Oh, yes," he said as if an afterthought. "It's below the burial site of Jesus, a poetic touch, don't you think?" He pulled out his cell phone to complete his part of the deal. At that moment, though, the front door burst open and three large men in leather jackets stormed in. Hassan's guard raised his Kalashnikov, but was gunned down before he could fire. The men spoke flawless English.

"Please sit down," one of them said. "We need only to keep you safe until midnight and then you will be free to go."

Hassan, Paola and I sat side by side on the green sofa. Hassan's face turned ashen. "We're fucked," he said.

The three men left us to ourselves, but never took their eyes off us. I was terrified. "Are they with the terrorists?" I asked Hassan.

He laughed nervously. "No, my dear, these are Israelis."

I tried to grasp the meaning of this. If they were Israelis why were they not asking where the bomb was? "Hassan, what's going on?"

Paola glared at Hassan. "What are they planning to do with us?" she asked.

Hassan took a deep breath, exhaled slowly. "They will hold us till the deadline, to hedge their bets, so to speak. Then, they will kill us. We know too much."

Chapter 37

Frank called Jill. She answered on the first ring, always calm and collected, except when her volcanic temper erupted. He quickly told her what he knew and what he suspected. It was getting uncomfortably close to the deadline, which Jill already knew had been set back to midnight. They had ordered the evacuation of the consular staff and all other Americans from the West Bank and Jerusalem, she explained, and she told Frank he should leave as well.

"I'm going to confront Ratner," he told her. "I'll call you from there."

"Frank, we are now leaning towards your theory, but we don't have enough to act on it. When a whole city is threatened with a nuclear apocalypse, we have to be sure. We need something more," she said.

"I'll get something from Ratner, if I have to torture him for it. What convinced you that I might be right?"

"That fingerprint the Saudi's found. Iran's President Rouhani called the President a few minutes ago and insisted they had nothing to do with this plot. The Revolutionary

Guard commander whose fingerprint was found in the wreckage of one of the vans in the attack was not retired, as we first thought. He was living in Peshawar and, according to Iranian intelligence, had spied for the Israelis when Chaim Ratner was running Mossad. Rouhani had extensive proof and he even exposed some operational details and secrets that convinced us he was telling the truth.

"What now?"

"The President is going to call the Prime Minister. We're worried they may order a preemptive strike. The pilots are in the cockpits and are ready to takeoff. It's very dangerous. They need our refueling capacity to establish any surprise, so we have some leverage. As for Jerusalem, they don't have the time anymore to evacuate the city. They pinned a lot of hope on that twelve-hour extension and now they're stuck. Call me before you see Ratner."

Frank hung up and asked his driver to take him back to the Knesset and the command center as fast as possible. But now the streets were in total gridlock as news of the US decision to evacuate its nationals from the Holy City created a viral panic. Frank tried repeatedly to call Celia, but there was no answer. He called Paola, same thing. He tried to stay calm, but his heart raced out of control. At the epicenter of a possible nuclear explosion, all Frank could think about was that Celia and Paola were in danger and he was not there to protect them. That, more than any bomb, was his greatest nightmare. He stopped dialing to save his battery.

When he finally made it to the Knesset, he rushed downstairs to the command center and was told that Ratner was in a closed meeting with the Prime Minister. He waited in a hallway on a metal chair watching the second hand of a large clock on the wall, counting each minute. When the meeting broke, he brushed past a circle of military brass and grabbed Ratner by the arm. "I've got to see you, right now," he demanded. "I have a message for you from our President."

"It's impossible," Ratner replied. He looked up at the clock. "We've only got thirty minutes before the bomb goes off."

"There is no bomb," Frank said in a low voice that no one else could hear.

Ratner stared into Frank's eyes with a look of fear and disgust. "Come, follow me," he said, grabbing General Lonzman on his way as he guided them into a secure room.

"I know everything," Frank told him, jumping right into it. "I know you hired Hassan Al-Kidwa. I know you created this whole Khybar Brigade from jihadists you recruited in Peshawar, probably through that Iranian spy whose fingerprints you so convincingly left at the scene of the attack at Sarghoda. I know you had Al-Kidwa travel to Tehran to make everyone think the Iranians were behind this. I know how you used Celia and Paola. I suspect your plan has always been to force the evacuation of Palestinians from the West Bank under the guise of protecting them to achieve your dream of a Greater Israel."

Ratner continued to glare at him with a smirk of superiority, as Frank continued. "The one thing I couldn't figure out was why you would risk bringing a nuclear weapon into Israel.

How could you be sure you could keep control of it, that one of the jihadists might not press the trigger? In fact, I assume you did lose control. You needed the extra twelve hours you had been offered to completely clear the West Bank."

Neither Lonzman nor Ratner displayed any reaction. Frank continued. "But I just came back from Hadassah Hospital. General Akram's wife showed me a letter her husband had sent her just before he killed himself, or perhaps was killed on your orders. I first suspected you were behind this plot when we learned that you had made the arrangements for Akram's wife to have a life-saving operation performed here. For all I know, you might even have been the cause of her illness. It doesn't matter. I knew Akram. He was a good man, a genuine nationalist. He wouldn't have given you plans that would have allowed you or anyone else to steal a real nuclear warhead, but a counterfeit one? Perhaps that price was not too great to save his wife's life. Letting you know when they would move the shill that he used to keep the Indians guessing was not so big a deal. What could one do with a fake bomb, except bluff?"

Ratner's diabolical smile was grotesque. "Perhaps you're right, Frank. But what if you're wrong? Maybe the bomb is real. Do you think my government will risk the lives of its people and our holy city for your hunch? Besides, there's one thing you don't know. When Ms. Ramirez brought you to Abu Dhabi, I realized there might be a problem. I've long admired your skills, so much so that I once tried to eliminate them in Beirut. But let bygones be bygones, I say. I considered we might face a situation like this, so I took some precautions.

219

I try to think of everything. He pulled his phone from his pocket and pressed one of the speed dials. "Put the dark-haired girl on," he said and handed the phone to Frank.

"Hello?" Frank recognized Celia's voice.

"Celia?"

"Frank. It's in the Church of the Holy…" But before she could say more, Ratner grabbed the phone away from him.

"I'm sorry, but you can chat later. Mr. Al-Kidwa and your friends are well protected, I can assure you. You've already lost your wife, I understood. I don't think you want to lose your future one."

Frank wanted to reach over and strangle Ratner, but he couldn't risk Celia and Paola's lives. Instead, he reached into his pocket for his cell phone. Thinking he was about to pull out a gun, General Lonzman unholstered his revolver from under his jacket. Frank smiled and held up his hand. "Jill? Did you get all that?"

"Sure did," said the voice on the other end.

Ratner had a look of disgust. "I'm afraid it's too late, Frank. Nothing can stop this now, not even your President. There are some very talented Israeli commandos preparing to blast their way into a vault deep under the Church of the Holy Sepulcher." He looked at his watch. "At any moment now. The bomb will be dismantled, the terrorists all killed, Hassan Al-Kidwa, the man who orchestrated this, will be gunned down in Abu Dhabi, and we will be the heroes who saved our people from a second holocaust. We have proof, even a written confession from Al-Kidwa that Iran financed and directed the whole plot, the 'Abraham Affair' as we call it. Our Air Force will take out their secret nuclear installations, which your President so negligently let them have, and remove any future threats."

The phone, still in Ratner's hand, rang. He held it to his ear. "Yes, yes, Mr. Prime Minister. I understand. Frank could easily hear the Prime Minister screaming in Hebrew. He was calling for an end to the evacuation and ordering the jets to turn off their engines."

General Lonzman raised his gun, looked at Frank and Ratner, put the nozzle to his temple and fired.

Ratner pressed the speed dial again. "Let the girls go," he said, "and finish with Mr. Al-Kidwa."

At that moment a team of Israeli commandos, faces smudged with black, blasted their way into the ancient grotto below the spot where Jesus was thought to have been buried before his resurrection, and brought an end to the Abraham Affair.

Acknowledgement

Editors are the unsung heroes of literature. If you read a work of fiction and can't stop turning the pages, you can bet that it was well edited by someone other than the author. I got my first taste of the editor's scalpel when my editor, Jane Rogers, cut out 10,000 words from my debut book, *Citizens Rising: Independent Journalism and the Spread of Democracy* (CUNY Journalism Press 2013), a non-fiction account of the role of media activists in recent history. I remember lying in a fetal position on the floor crying at the loss of what Stephen King calls the "little darlings." We writers get real attached to our progeny. In my most recent novel, Jane had me remove seven chapters. Ouch! But one gets used to it when we realize how much stronger the book becomes. It takes someone of great strength of character to speak truth to authors and an exquisite ear. Jane Rogers has both of these in surplus. But it is not only the art of excision. As my editor, she also contributed significantly to plot and character development. I feel the most profound debt of gratitude to Jane, who is in every sense of the word my partner. If my books have any value, a lot of the credit must go to her.

www.ingramcontent.com/pod-product-compliance
Lightning Source LLC
Chambersburg PA
CBHW031241120726
47905CB00002B/678